RUNNING SCARED

Leslie McGill

SADDLEBACK
EDUCATIONAL PUBLISHING

CAP CENTRAL

Fighter
Running Scared
Hacker

SADDLEBACK
EDUCATIONAL PUBLISHING
www.sdlback.com

ISBN-13: 978-1-62250-706-1
ISBN-10: 1-62250-706-1
eBook: 978-1-61247-957-6

Printed in Guangzhou, China
NOR/1014/CA21401625

18 17 16 15 14   2 3 4 5 6

To Jordy and Nathan, with love.

RAINIE

Rainie stood on the edge of her bed. The small wall mirror showed only the middle of her five-foot-seven frame. Turning sideways, she looked at her butt. It still stuck out. No matter how much weight she lost, she still looked fat. She wished she hadn't eaten that piece of chicken at dinner last night. She had only eaten half of it. And she hadn't touched the mashed potatoes or corn. But she shouldn't have given in to her hunger.

She used to love her mom's fried chicken. But that seemed a lifetime ago. Back when her dad was still around. Before her mom started working at DC's Bar and Grill. Before Daymon Jenkins started hanging out at their house. Commenting on Rainie's figure. Looking her up and down, even while he was pawing her mother.

Before Rainie started locking her bedroom door at night.

Before she decided to become invisible.

What she saw in the mirror made her feel sick. She'd simply have to keep losing weight. She pulled out the scale she had hidden under her bed and stepped on it. Down to one hundred two pounds. But if she leaned on it, the needle moved a bit toward the right. Rainie shook her head in disgust. If she was going to lose this fat, she just couldn't eat anything today.

She carefully slid the scale back under her bed. She leaned forward to look at her face in the mirror. Strange. Her skin had gotten really dry, but her face had been breaking out more than usual lately. Her hair seemed to be drying out too. When she tried to style it, she would find clumps that had fallen onto her dresser.

She pulled on some warm-up pants and a long-sleeved T-shirt. Then she layered another T-shirt on top of that. Despite the Washington, D.C., heat and humidity, she always seemed to be cold.

"You still looking in that mirror?" her mother

yelled up the stairs. "Rainie Burkette, how many times I got to tell you—"

Rainie started down the hall.

"Man, hard to believe she can even see herself in that mirror, skinny as she is," she heard Daymon say.

As she made her way down the stairs, she stopped to listen.

"I don't know what to do with her," her mother said with a dramatic sigh. "I've been cooking same as always. She says she's just not hungry."

"Used to have some meat on her," Daymon said. "Had herself a cute little shape. Now she's some scrawny thing. Looks like a scarecrow. Look like she has some disease or something."

Rainie's heart soared at his words. It was working! If she could just get skinny enough, maybe he would quit looking at her the way he did.

She heard a chair scrape on the floor. "But now her mama's a different story!" he said with a dirty laugh. "Her mama's got something here and here and—"

"Oh, Daymon, stop!" her mother said in a little girl voice, giggling. "Not with the girls still here!"

Rainie knew the silence that followed meant that her mother and Daymon were kissing.

Jesika's bedroom was at the top of the stairs. Rainie glanced up as her door opened. The nine-year-old pretended to throw up as she walked to the bathroom. Rainie clapped her hand across her mouth to keep from laughing. She thumped loudly down the remaining steps.

"Okay, I'm leaving," Rainie said, walking into the kitchen as if she hadn't heard anything.

Her mother broke away from Daymon, looking guilty. Her face was flushed and her hair was untidy. She was still in her nightgown, which clung to her curves and was cut low.

Rainie looked away in disgust. Since meeting Daymon, her mother had changed. Almost overnight, her mother had turned trampy. She wore clothes that were too tight and too young. She didn't even try to hide that she and Daymon were fooling around.

Rainie knew that her mother was badly hurt when their dad left. Ever since the divorce, the mom she knew was gone. The mom who always had time to listen to her girls and was there for them. In her place was a cheap-looking stranger who only had time for Daymon. Rainie couldn't remember the last time she'd had an actual conversation with her mother about anything. All they seemed to talk about was upcoming plans. She desperately missed her "real" mom and hated this new cheap version.

Rainie knew that Daymon was the reason her mother started dressing like she did. She suspected it was because Daymon was so much younger than her mother. Besides the changes he'd caused in her mother, there was another reason Rainie hated Daymon.

He scared her. When he was in the house, Rainie was always aware of him. He followed her with his eyes whenever she walked. He also touched her. A lot. Pretending that these touches were accidental. Sometimes, when she was in the bathroom, she could hear him outside the door.

She tried telling her mother once how he made her feel. The conversation didn't go well.

"Honey, you're getting old enough to

understand that men're gonna look all they want. It's what they do. And the more they look, the better you know *you're* looking. I don't understand why you'd want him to stop. Just shows how pretty you've gotten."

"Mom, he's your boyfriend! I don't like him looking at me."

It was at that point that the conversation took an ugly turn. "Well, what are you doing that's making him watch you so much? You tryin' to catch his eye?"

Rainie was crushed. Her mother should have backed her up, not blamed her. Rainie decided she would do all she could to try to be invisible. She stayed in her room as much as she could, coming out only when her mother made her join them for dinner or when she was leaving the house.

And she quit eating.

Not eating made her feel strong. As if she—and only she—had power over her body. But not eating hadn't taken the weight off fast enough. So she started running. One thought kept her going: the calories she was burning off. But no matter what she did, she never felt that she looked thin enough. She'd lost more than twenty-five pounds since the summer. But when she looked at herself, she still thought she looked fat.

She wondered about the other changes she'd noticed lately. Her ratty hair and skin problems. She kept thinking that her skin was breaking out because she was getting her period. But so far, nothing. In fact, she couldn't remember the last time she'd had a period. She wondered if running could be having an effect on her cycle. She made a mental note to look it up on the Internet the next time she was on a school computer.

She grabbed her backpack from the floor where she'd left it when she came in late last night. She hoped her mother hadn't noticed. She always did her homework in her room, so the backpack still in the kitchen meant she hadn't done any work. Again. But with working at FreeZees, a frozen yogurt shop, and running, she never seemed to have time to study anymore.

But her mother didn't notice the backpack. "You aren't wearing all those layers!" her mother said in horror. "In this heat? What's wrong with you lately? You comin' down with somethin'?"

"I get cold in class. They have the air conditioning turned way up," Rainie lied. She suspected that if her mother saw her arms and legs, she'd be worried. Although Rainie looked fat to herself, other people had started commenting on how skinny she looked.

"Wait, you haven't eaten any breakfast!" her mother said in a worried tone. "Rainie, you got to eat. I could make you something."

"C'mon, Gabby, she's fine, she's just fine," Daymon said. "Back when I was working at Coolidge, most kids just ate breakfast at school." Daymon used to be the janitor at a neighboring high school. Rainie had once asked her mother why he didn't work there anymore. But her mother got angry, accusing Rainie of being nosy. Rainie suspected that her mom didn't know why Daymon had lost his job.

Daymon put his hand on Rainie's mother's hip and looked at Rainie with an evil smile. "Time for you to go, girl, and give us some privacy!"

Rainie felt sick at the disrespectful way he treated her mother. "I'll eat at school," she lied, ignoring Daymon. "I don't want to be late," she added, kissing her mother's cheek and heading for the door.

"Ain't you gonna kiss me good-bye?" Daymon said with a leer.

In your dreams, creep, Rainie thought. She didn't even look his way. "I'm working at FreeZees after school, so I'll see you later, Mom."

"Okay, baby," her mother said. And then, "Daymon, stop! Not yet. Jessie's still here."

Rainie slammed the door as hard as she could.

JOSS

The door to the run-down row house on Seventeenth Street burst open. Rainie Burkette ran out and slammed the door hard behind her. Joss White had never seen her look so angry.

"Hey, girl!" Joss said in surprise. "Who messed with *your* Wheaties this morning?"

Rainie shook her head angrily. "Nobody important, that's for sure," she said.

Joss looked at her curiously. Joss and Rainie had always been friendly, but they had become close last summer when they both worked at FreeZees. Joss had quit the yogurt shop in August. Since then, they hadn't spent as much time together.

She was shocked at the change in Rainie's appearance. She had always been pretty and well dressed. But now she looked awful. Her hair was pulled back into a sloppy ponytail. Her skin was a mess. Strangest of all was the way she was dressed. It was already over seventy degrees, but she was wearing sweatpants, a long-sleeved T-shirt, and another tee over that one. By the time school was out that afternoon, the D.C. heat and humidity were going to be brutal.

"You okay?" Joss asked with concern. "You know it's gonna be hot today, right?"

"Yeah, I'm fine," Rainie said. "I just threw on whatever was clean."

"But didn't you wear sweats yesterday too?" Joss asked. "I wondered why you didn't pass out in science lab. It was so hot in there!"

"I'm okay. Okay?" Rainie snapped. "Since when is it your job to keep track of what I wear every day?"

"Whoa! Hold up," Joss said. "I was just asking."

Rainie shook her head. "Sorry," she said. "I'm just a little tired from work."

They started walking down Seventeenth Street toward Capital Central High School, in the northeast quadrant of Washington, D.C.

"So you worked last night?" Joss asked.

"Yeah, you know how that goes," Rainie lied. "Angie is once again short-handed, so ..."

"I am so glad I'm out of FreeZees," Joss said. "Angie is a good manager, but I would be absolutely flunking out if I had to work *plus* keep my grades up. You're so lucky. I wish I was half as smart as you."

Rainie had always been one of the smartest students Joss knew. While Joss struggled to maintain her grades, Rainie was always placed in accelerated and honors courses.

"Hey, Joss. Rainie. Wait up!" Joss and Rainie turned and saw Eva Morales hurrying toward them. Eva and Joss had been best friends since elementary school.

"What the—" Eva said, stopping suddenly when she reached the others. "Girl, have you checked the calendar?" she said to Rainie. "You're dressed like winter!"

"Why is everyone so concerned about the way I'm dressed this morning?" Rainie asked angrily. "Just because I'm not showing half my butt like—"

Joss and Eva looked at each other. Both were wearing shorts. Joss's were as short as the school would allow, showing off her long, slender legs. Eva's came down to right above her knees. She often wore baggy clothes to cover up how overweight she was.

"Guess she means you," Eva joked to Joss, trying to lighten the mood.

"I guess so," Joss said coldly. Rainie's words had hurt. Joss didn't know what was going on, but something clearly was up.

The three girls walked on in an uncomfortable silence. From behind them, someone whistled. They stopped and waited as Lionel "Ferg" Ferguson, Carlos Garcia, and Durand Butler rounded the corner from L Street. Carlos threw his arm around Joss and kissed her. They'd been together for several years but had broken up for about a year when Carlos's family had moved to Virginia when his father had been ill. Now that he was back, they were closer than ever.

Joss buried her face in his chest.

"Hey, what's this?" he asked. "Everything okay?"

"Yeah, fine," Joss said. She was still hurt by Rainie's comment.

Ferg put his arm around Eva and gave her a quick kiss. They'd been going out for a year. Like Eva, Ferg was large. He was one of Cap Central High School's star football players. The two of them took up the whole sidewalk.

"Hey, you want one too?" Durand Butler said. He put his arm around Rainie's neck and kissed the top of her head.

She was so shocked she didn't move. Just stared at him with her eyes wide.

"Didn't want you to feel left out!" Durand said with a smile. Like the other guys, he was wearing shorts and a T-shirt. Just walking up the street had made him sweat.

He stood back and looked her up and down. "Girl, aren't you dying from the heat?"

"Don't ask!" Joss and Eva said in unison.

Rainie rolled her eyes. "Sorry, you guys," she said. "I'm just a little touchy this morning, I guess."

"You sick?" Durand said, putting his hand on Rainie's forehead.

They all started walking to school. Joss and Carlos led the way, followed by Durand and Rainie, with Eva and Ferg in the rear.

"I don't know if *she's* sick, but I'm sure sick of her act," Joss whispered to Carlos. "I've only been with her about five minutes, and she's already snapped at me a million times."

"A million, huh?" Carlos said with a smile. "And for once you're not exaggerating, right?"

"Okay, maybe not a million, but at least three," Joss whispered hotly. "Shhh. I want to hear what they're talking about."

"You are such a snoop!" Carlos said. He started laughing.

"Did you understand that math homework last night?" Rainie was asking Durand.

"I finally figured it out, but it was hard," Durand said. "I was up late trying to finish."

"That's what you get for running so late!" Rainie said.

Durand looked surprised. "How did you know that?" he asked.

"You actually ran past me," Rainie said. "On Mount Olivet Road. By the cemetery."

"What?" Joss whispered to Carlos. "No

wonder she's tired! She ran after she worked a shift at FreeZees."

"Why not?" Carlos said.

"Because it would have been eleven o'clock at night!" Joss said. "Who runs in D.C. that late? Is she out of her mind?"

"Maybe she—" Carlos started.

"Shhh. Let me listen," Joss said.

Carlos rolled his eyes.

"Sorry, I never saw you," Durand said. "I must have been in the zone. What were you doing over there?"

"Running. I ran past you on the other side of the street," Rainie said.

Joss couldn't stand it anymore. She turned around so abruptly that Durand nearly walked into her.

"Wait!" she said to Rainie. "You said you worked last night."

Rainie looked guilty. "Uh, I don't think so," she said. "You must have misunderstood."

Joss put a hand on her hip as she looked skeptically at Rainie. She knew she was right. "Whatever," she said under her breath.

She turned back to Carlos. "Rainie's lying,"

Joss whispered to him. "Something's up with her, but I don't know what it is."

"Why would she lie about working?" Carlos asked. "Why the big secret?"

"I don't know," Joss said. "But she looks terrible, don't you think?"

"She's probably just miserable about being so hot," Carlos said. "Who dresses like that at this time of year?"

"I know, right?" Joss agreed. "Something's just not right."

RAINIE

Do you work out even when it's not wrestling season?" Rainie asked Durand.

"Pretty much, or I get really out of shape," he said. "You run a lot?"

"A bit," Rainie said. She didn't want Durand or anyone else to know how important running had become. Running was her way of working off any calories she'd eaten during the day. It was also a way of occupying her time so she wouldn't be tempted to eat. Best of all, it kept her away from home—and Daymon.

"You want to run together some time?" Durand asked. "How far do you run anyway?"

"About five miles a night," Rainie said. "Give or take. Except on the nights I work."

"Five miles?" Durand asked in horror. "Girl,

what's wrong with you? You training for a marathon?"

"Something like that," Rainie said.

"When do you study?" Durand asked curiously.

"After I get back from running," Rainie said, lying again. Lately, she just never seemed to have the energy to study. Her grades showed it. She had always been able to pull off nearly perfect grades without trying too hard. The Cs she was getting lately were upsetting. She had hidden her report card from her mother. Luckily, her mom was so wrapped up in Daymon that she had forgotten to ask about it. But Rainie knew it was just a matter of time.

They arrived at Cap Central, and Durand held the door open for her. "You want to grab some breakfast?" he asked, turning toward the cafeteria. A large crowd of kids was lining up to select their food.

"Nah, I'm good," Rainie said. "See you in math."

The smell of breakfast coming out of the cafeteria made her mouth water. She had to get away before she'd be tempted to eat anything. She started toward the stairs.

"Hey, Rainie!"

Rainie turned around and waited for Eva and Joss to catch up.

"What's up?" she asked.

"You want to get some breakfast?" Joss asked.

"Nah, I ate before I left," Rainie lied again.

"That what you were so mad about?" Joss said with a laugh. "Someone drink all the orange juice?"

"Something like that," Rainie said. "Thanks, though. That's the second invitation to breakfast I've gotten today."

"I think we can guess who the first one was from," Eva said, grinning. "But actually, I wanted to ask you guys something. Did you hear that Cap Central's going to have a poms team?"

"Poms? What are poms?" Rainie asked.

"They're like a dance team but with pom-poms. They perform at games, pep rallies, all sorts of events. Cardozo High School has a poms team. I saw them when we played them last year. It looks like lots of fun."

"I'd like that more than cheering," Joss said. "I can't do those flips or splits that the cheerleaders do. But shake pom-poms? I could do that!"

"You'd have to shake more than your pom-poms, girl," Eva said. "There's some dancing too, so you can guess what you'd be shaking. Mrs. McArdle is the advisor. She wants to meet at lunch today with anyone who's interested."

"Oh, she's nice," Joss said. "I had her for sophomore English."

"I actually have her this year," Rainie said. "She's teaching one junior English class."

"I heard she's tough," Eva said. "She never cuts anyone a break on grades, even if it means they get suspended from their team. You heard what she did to Marcus DiMonte, right? Kept him from playing basketball until he got his grades up. So how about you, Rainie?" Eva asked. "You in?"

It did sound like fun. "Sure. When and where?" she asked.

"At lunch in Mrs. McArdle's classroom," Eva said. "Let's meet in the cafeteria and bring our lunches upstairs."

"Sounds good," Rainie said. She knew she wouldn't show up in the cafeteria. She'd go straight to Mrs. McArdle's class and pretend she had misunderstood.

The said their good-byes. Then the girls all went in opposite directions.

At the top of the stairs, she ran into Mrs. McArdle.

"How you coming with that Shakespeare project, Rainie?" she asked.

"I'm working on it," Rainie lied. She hadn't started the project, which was worth twenty-five percent of her grade.

"Well, don't put it off," Mrs. McArdle said, walking down the hall to her classroom. "You know it's due next week. No exceptions."

"Right," Rainie said, walking toward her first class. Just then her cell phone buzzed with a text message. It was from Angie Stewart, manager at FreeZees.

"Corie needs wkend off. Can u work 2-nite, Fri, Sat, and Sun—pls?"

Sure, she thought, *why not? Anything to keep me out of the house.*

Rainie's empty stomach tightened with tension. Her fear about Daymon was constantly on her mind. It was there when she was supposed to be studying. It was there when she was in her house. It was what made her hit the streets, running her heart out. Her grades were slipping, she was starting to look really rough, and she barely had enough energy to climb the stairs at school. But she didn't have any other choice. There was no way out.

CHAPTER 4

JOSS

Joss and Eva went to the cafeteria as soon as the lunch bell rang. They got their trays and looked around for Rainie.

"I don't think she's coming," Joss said. "We'd better go or we'll be late."

"Maybe she misunderstood us," Eva said. "I'll bet she's already in Mrs. McArdle's room."

"She may be up there, but not because she misunderstood," Joss said. "She's really acting odd. You know she lied to me this morning."

"About what?" Eva said.

"About something stupid. She absolutely told me she had been working last night. She said that's why she looked so rough this morning. Then when she started talking to Durand, she said she was out running late last night. I heard her tell him she runs five miles a night. You can't do that and work each night at the yogurt shop. So she's lying about something— either running or working."

"That doesn't make any sense," Eva said. "Why would she lie? Do you think she was trying to impress him?"

"No, just the opposite," Joss said. They started for the stairs. "I think she was telling *him* the truth. I think she lied to *me* about working. But I can't figure out why."

"I wonder what happened to her," Eva said. "She looked good this summer. But she looks awful now. Like she's homeless or something. Do you think it's because the family is broke since her dad bailed on them?"

"It's possible," Joss said. "That row house they live in looks like it should be condemned. But I feel like there's more going on. Something serious. And I'm going to figure out what it is."

They walked into Mrs. McArdle's room. Rainie was sitting in the front row.

"Hey, where were you?" Eva said. "We waited for you in the cafeteria."

"Oh, sorry!" Rainie said. "Is that where we

were supposed to meet? I thought we were meeting up here."

"Really?" Joss said. Her tone made it clear that she didn't believe her.

Fortunately, right then Mrs. McArdle told everyone to take their seats. Besides Joss and Eva, there were eight other girls.

"All right, let's get started," Mrs. McArdle said. "For some time now, I've been thinking that this school needs to have a poms team. Poms are just like drill teams or dance teams but they use pom-poms."

"So when would we perform?" Joss asked. "Like at sporting events?"

"Right. Football games, basketball games, pep rallies. And depending on how you all feel about it, you could even compete. Competitive dance is getting to be really big, and we don't have a dance team."

"What would we wear?" Eva asked, looking worried. "I just can't see myself in a skanky little two-piece!"

"That would be up to you," Mrs. McArdle said. "But even if the uniform is two pieces, it doesn't have to be skanky. Some teams wear tank tops and shorts, others wear little skirts. You'll have to raise money for uniforms, so it might be a year or two before you have official-looking outfits. Until that time, you could just choose matching shorts and T-shirts."

"Will we have to try out?" asked Keisha Jackson, the student government association president.

"I don't see why," Mrs. McArdle said. "There aren't that many of you, so there's no competition for slots—yet. In a year or two, we may have to hold tryouts. But let's just assume you're all in. How's that?"

Her announcement was met with a buzz of excitement.

"Girls, girls! We don't have much time," Mrs. McArdle said, holding her hand up for silence. "I've made a list of things to think about before our next meeting." She passed out photocopied lists. "Let's get together in the small gym next Monday after school. Wear shorts and a T-shirt. Be prepared for a workout."

The other girls gathered up their lunch trash and threw it out on the way out of the classroom.

Rainie continued to sit at the desk.

"You coming?" Eva asked.

"Actually, I have Mrs. McArdle next period, so I'm just gonna stay," Rainie said.

"You didn't eat anything. You want my chips?" Joss asked.

"No, I'm good," Rainie answered. "I ate on the way up here."

A suspicious look crossed Joss's face. "Really?" she asked.

"Yes, Joss, *really*," Rainie repeated. "Something wrong?"

"I don't know. Running five miles a night, no breakfast, not meeting us at lunch, no chips—you training for something?" Joss asked.

"*Did* eat breakfast, *did* eat lunch, just didn't want the chips," Rainie mimicked. "Not training for anything. Just keepin' in shape."

Joss thought Rainie sounded more confident than she looked. She had found a small hole in her sweatpants and was poking a finger in and out of it in a nervous manner.

"I could not go through the day without eating," Eva confessed. She seemed oblivious to the tension between Joss and Rainie. "It is truly the highlight of my day. No wonder you're so skinny."

"But I'm not!" Rainie said forcefully. "I mean, I'm still really fat."

Joss couldn't believe what she was hearing. For a moment, she couldn't even speak.

"Where?" she finally asked incredulously.

"You'd be surprised," Rainie said.

"I'll take those chips if no one else wants them," Eva said.

Joss rolled her eyes and even Rainie laughed.

"Although I shouldn't," Eva said. "My butt is ready to get its own zip code!"

The bell rang, and Joss and Eva left.

RAINIE

Rainie, I need you to stay after class for a few minutes so I can talk to you," Mrs. McArdle said.

"Sure," Rainie answered. She was a little worried. Teachers usually didn't ask her to stay after class.

The door opened and the other students streamed in. Almost immediately, there was a loud crash. A desk toppled over sideways. Mrs. McArdle whirled around to see what had happened.

Luther Ransome and Chance Ruffin were giving each other high-fives while JaQuel Rivas picked up the desk. Rainie knew that either Luther or Chance had knocked it over. They were both athletes, and other students treated them like gods. JaQuel wouldn't tell on them, even if it meant he took the blame.

"Who knocked over that desk? Chance? Luther?" Mrs. McArdle asked.

"Um, sorry, Mrs. McArdle. I tripped. I'm a little clumsy," JaQuel mumbled.

"Okay, settle down. Take your seats please," Mrs. McArdle said. "First of all, there are a couple of students I need to talk to after class is over. Rainie Burkette, Thomas Porter, Luther Ransome, and Chance Ruffin, please stay after class. Now, let's get back to reading Shakespeare's *Richard III*. Who wants to read the part of Richard?"

When she heard the other students Mrs. McArdle needed to talk to, Rainie knew it wouldn't be good news. It was a new experience to be grouped with people like them. Thomas Porter was a thug who had just transferred to Cap Central after being expelled from a neighboring school. Luther Ransome and Chance Ruffin barely kept their athletic eligibility each year.

When class was over, the other students headed for the door. As they passed by Mrs. McArdle, she handed them their graded tests.

"Okay, I wanted to talk to the four of you because you all seem to be struggling in this class," Mrs. McArdle said when the rest of the students had left. She handed each of them their test. Rainie was stunned. At the top was a big red F.

"I need to know if you don't understand the material. Or are you just not doing the work?" Mrs. McArdle said.

"Thomas? Let's start with you."

"This sucks. I'm outta here," Thomas said, heading for the door.

"Thomas. You're going to fail English if you don't—" Mrs. McArdle stopped talking when the door slammed with a bang.

"Luther? Chance? Anything to say?"

Luther Ransome and Chance Ruffin were both smirking as they looked at the Fs on their tests. Neither seemed worried.

"I know you both play sports for Cap Central. You do know that if you fail this class, you'll lose your eligibility and not be able to play, don't you?"

"Yeah, well, we ain't worried," Luther said.

"No? And why is that?" Mrs. McArdle asked.

" 'Cause it's all good," he said. "We got it covered."

Beside him, Chance laughed hard. Rainie couldn't believe they would joke about a failing grade. Her stomach felt like it was tied in a knot. The F at the top of her paper stood out like a neon light. She was humiliated.

"Well, I hope your plan includes doing well on the Shakespeare assignment due next week. Because I am warning you, I will not cut you a break on your grade. If you fail, you fail—and remember that you cannot graduate from high school if you don't pass English."

Both boys continued to smirk. Luther got up, and Chance got to his feet as well. "It'll be fine, Mrs. McArdle," Luther said. "Just chill."

The two walked out of the room, and the door clicked behind them.

"So that leaves you, Rainie," Mrs. McArdle said. "I was shocked when I graded your test. So I checked out your grades in other classes. You're barely passing. And before this year, I don't think you'd ever seen a grade lower than a B, had you?"

Rainie shook her head in discouragement.

"Tell me what's going on with you," Mrs. McArdle asked kindly. "This isn't like you. I don't have a class this period. I can write you a pass to excuse you being late to your next class. Talk to me."

For a moment, Rainie thought about telling Mrs. McArdle about Daymon. But she knew she couldn't. Last year, a Cap Central girl had told a school counselor that her mother's boyfriend had touched her inappropriately. The girl was put in foster care. Rainie couldn't risk being separated from Jesika. She shook her head slowly.

"Okay, I understand you might not want to talk about it. But I'm wondering if you're doing too much these days. You don't look very healthy. Do you have a job? Sports? What's taking up your time since I don't think much of it is being spent studying?"

Rainie told her about FreeZees and running, but she knew they sounded like lame excuses. Almost without being able to help herself, Rainie said, "Am I going to be able to join poms?"

"I'd love to have you on the team. In fact, I'd hoped you would be one of the leaders," Mrs. McArdle said. "But you need to do your part. You have to have a C-average to be eligible. When I checked your grades, they were below that.

Midterm grades won't be posted until next week. Is there anything you can do to get your grades up by then?"

"I can try," Rainie said. She didn't know how. She just felt like giving up.

"Look, Rainie, I'm not stupid," Mrs. McArdle said. "I know there's something you're not telling me. You're a different girl than you were even a couple of months ago. I really, really wish you'd trust me enough to let me try to help. You seem like a person who needs someone to talk to."

Rainie started gathering her books. "No, I'm fine," she lied. "I'm just tired, that's all."

Mrs. McArdle looked disappointed for a minute, but then she went back to looking all business-like. "Well, I hope you've got time for poms. It's a big commitment."

"I can do it," Rainie said. "And I'm sorry about the test. I'll try to do better."

"I know you will," Mrs. McArdle said as she filled out Rainie's late pass. "Rainie, sometimes when things aren't going well in your life, you need to take action to make them better. It's hard to know what to do when you're feeling scared or confused. That's when talking to someone else can help. Remember what I said. I'm here if you need me."

Rainie felt tears spring to her eyes. She looked away so Mrs. McArdle couldn't see them. "Okay," she mumbled as she grabbed her pass and walked out of the room. "Thanks."

JOSS

When Joss got to science class, she looked around. Rainie's seat was empty. She wondered where she was.

Mrs. Reed told the class to meet with their science fair partners. Joss and Eva took their usual seats at the lab table closest to the door.

"Where do you think Rainie is?" Eva asked.

"No clue," Joss answered. "I wonder if she went home sick."

"She looked okay at the poms meeting," Eva answered.

Right then the door opened and Rainie walked in. She handed Mrs. Reed a pass and joined Joss and Eva at the lab table.

"Where were you?" Joss asked.

"I had to go over some stuff with Mrs. McArdle," Rainie answered.

"School stuff?" Joss pushed.

"Of course," Rainie said. She looked away as she said it. As if she was lying. "Anyway, you want to talk about our project?"

The three girls were working together on a science fair project, testing whether antibacterial soap really prevented bacteria from growing.

"Okay, here's the progress report," Eva said. "Really, truly disgusting scum is growing on some of our bowls of chicken soup. My mother is getting tired of having to move them out of the way in order to do the laundry. So we'd better finish this up pretty soon, or I'm afraid she's going to dump them down the drain."

"Okay, end of progress report," Joss said. "Now let's talk about poms!"

"I thought it sounded like fun," Rainie said. "And I like the other girls who showed up."

"I thought the same thing," Joss agreed. "I think it will be great."

"Hey, you guys want to sleep over on Saturday?" Eva asked. "We can work on science for a while and maybe talk about poms. But mostly we can just hang."

"Sounds good," Joss answered.

"Can't," Rainie said. "I have to work."

"Tell Angie you have to get your schoolwork done," Joss urged her. "She's okay about stuff like that."

"I'll try, but Corie already said she wasn't coming in, so I may not have a choice."

"Carlos told me that he and Ferg and the others are going to be working on their project too. Maybe we can all get together for a study break," Joss said. "And say, Miss Rainie," she added in a teasing voice. "Don't think we didn't all see hot Mister Durand Butler kissing you this morning! Something you want to tell us about what's going on with you two?"

"Nothing to tell," Rainie said. "I've known Durand forever. He just didn't want me to feel left out since you and Eva were getting some action. So he went ahead and gave me a kiss."

Joss and Eva laughed.

"So that was a mercy kiss?" Eva asked. "So kind of him!"

"Trust me, that's all it was," Rainie said. She seemed a little uncomfortable with the teasing.

"We should make sure he comes over Saturday night, don't you think?" Joss said to Eva. "If you're going to be there," she said to Rainie.

"I'll do my best," Rainie said. "Now can we talk about the project?"

"All work, as always," Eva grumbled. "But yeah. Let's decide who's doing what. I'll paste all the stuff on the display board. I'm no good with graphs or research or whatever, so I'll leave that to you geniuses."

For the rest of the period, they talked about science.

CHAPTER 7

RAINIE

When school ended, Rainie left Capital Central and began walking down Bladensburg Road toward FreeZees. From behind her, someone called her name. She turned and waited as Durand Butler caught up with her.

"Hi!" she said. She was glad to see him. He looked good and smelled kind of sweaty—but in a good way.

"Where you headed?" he asked.

"H Street. I work at FreeZees," she said.

"Oh man, I could never work there. I love frozen yogurt so much. If I worked there, I'd never make weight, and I'd get kicked off the team. How do you resist it?"

"I'm used to it now," Rainie said. "At first it was hard, but now it doesn't bother me." She wouldn't tell him that her self-control was an obsession. "How about you? What are you doing over here?"

"I'm meeting the guys at Primo's for pizza," Durand said.

"Now that's a place I couldn't work!" Rainie said with a laugh. "The smell of pepperoni would do me in."

"I used to see you there with your folks," Durand said. "Does your family still eat there?"

Rainie laughed bitterly. "Actually, my family's not much of a family anymore," she said. "My dad left about a year ago. And now my mom has this boyfriend ..."

"And?" Durand said, looking at her.

"And he's awful!" Rainie said louder than she meant to. "Really, really awful," she added quietly, her voice cracking.

"In what way?" Durand asked.

"He, he ..." her voice trailed off. She had been about to say, "He scares me," but she caught herself just in time. She couldn't let anyone know what was happening at the Burkette's house.

Durand waited a moment. "He's that great, huh?" he chuckled.

Rainie just shook her head, then she laughed too. "Know how sometimes people say 'it's better than nothing'? Well, compared to this guy, 'nothing' would be a relief."

"Well, maybe your mom will figure it out," Durand said. "Meanwhile, why don't you Google him to see if there's anything you should know about him. Maybe you could persuade your mom that way."

"That's not a bad idea," Rainie said thoughtfully.

They stopped at the door of FreeZees.

"Here we are, I guess," Durand said. "Do you wear a uniform?"

"Yes," Rainie groaned. "A white visor and a bright green apron. Very sophisticated."

"I can't wait to see it. I'll stop in when I'm leaving Primo's. You running tonight?"

"Probably not. I won't get out of here until ten."

"Some other time, then. Don't work too hard!"

Rainie waved good-bye and opened the door to FreeZees. She put on her apron and visor and got to work.

A little while later she heard the roar of a car's engine. A black Escalade pulled up to the curb. Luther Ransome and Chance Ruffin came into the shop. They grabbed bowls and began filling them.

"Whoops!" Luther said as the soft frozen yogurt spilled out over the top of the bowl. Leaving the mess, he walked over to the toppings. He scooped up M&Ms with his hand and began eating them.

"Hey, you can't eat from there!" Rainie called out from behind the cash register.

"So what'd McArdle say?" Luther asked as he walked toward the scale. He picked up a plastic spoon and started eating the yogurt.

"Same thing as to you," Rainie answered. "Get my grades up or else."

"Well, girl, I got mine covered." Luther laughed. "It's all in who you know!"

"And what's that supposed to mean?" Rainie asked.

"I got something going on. That Shakespeare assignment is being written while we speak."

"What? By who?" Rainie asked. Luther was one of those bad boys that some girls couldn't resist. She had no doubt that one of them was writing his Shakespeare paper for him.

"Don't you worry about that," Luther said. "And anyway, maybe I'm doing the assignment myself."

"Yeah, right!" Rainie said. "I just wonder who Chance is going to find to write his paper."

Chance tipped his yogurt cup upside down, and the sticky mess spilled on the floor. Luther laughed and refilled his own cup. He then headed for the door.

"Hey! You have to pay for that," she called.

"Put it on my tab," Luther said, laughing, as the little bell on the door tinkled. The two boys got into the Escalade and roared away with a squeal.

Rainie sighed in disgust. Great. She'd have to replace the entire container of M&Ms after Luther stuck his grimy hand in them. She grabbed a mop to clean up Chance's mess.

JOSS

After school, Joss waited for Carlos by the trophy case. Her mother was a member of the D.C. City Council and often had evening meetings. Joss usually made herself something for dinner, but tonight she wanted to hang out at Primo's.

"Hey, hot thing!" Carlos said when he finally showed up. "Sorry, I had to talk to Mrs. Blackwell about that SAT course I might take. So how was the rest of your day?"

Joss got up from where she was sitting on the floor doing her homework.

"Okay, but I'm even more worried about Rainie," Joss said.

They left through the side door on Bladensburg Road and walked toward H Street.

"What now?" Carlos asked.

"She's just acting weird," Joss said. "She said she'd meet us at lunch but didn't show up. She said she thought we were supposed to meet in Mrs. McArdle's room. But we had made it really clear that we were going to meet in the cafeteria so we could get some food."

"So maybe she just has a lot on her mind," Carlos said. "It's not a big mistake, right?"

"But that's not all," Joss said. "She said she ate her lunch on the way to Mrs. McArdle's room. But I know she didn't. I don't know how, but I'm certain she didn't eat anything. And she didn't eat breakfast with us either. She said she ate at home. But I can't believe she brought her lunch. Last year, she always ate a school lunch. And I'd put money on her family not having much to eat at home."

"Well, it does—" Carlos started.

"Oh," Joss added, "she's wearing sweats and two T-shirts. In this heat. It's so wrong."

"It does seem like a lot of little lies," Carlos said thoughtfully. "What, exactly, do you think her problem is? You know her lots better than me, so I can't see any change."

"My best guess?" Joss said. "She's got some

sort of eating disorder. I don't know if she's making herself throw up, but she's lost a ton of weight. And she's deliberately not eating with us. I started thinking, have you ever seen her in the cafeteria this year? Because I haven't. Put that with the lying, and it tells me that something serious is going on."

"Is she better friends with Eva? Would Rainie say what was wrong if Eva asked?" Carlos asked.

Joss was quiet for a moment. "I don't see that happening," she said finally. "You know I love Eva—she's been my best friend forever. But she's not always real observant. Or sensitive. She's great, don't get me wrong. But she hasn't even noticed a problem. And if she asked Rainie if she was okay, and Rainie said yes, I think Eva would believe her. She doesn't look into things too deeply."

"While you, on the other hand, are always suspecting that there's more going on than meets the eye," Carlos said kindly. "It's one of the things I love about you. But sometimes ..."

"I know, I see things that aren't even there," Joss said. "Like when you were about to move, and I thought you were breaking up with me. Although I was right that something was wrong. I was wrong about what it was."

They walked into Primo's. "So what are you going to do?" he asked.

"I don't know yet," Joss said. "She needs to talk to someone. But she won't talk to me. I need to figure out who she will open up to."

"Hey! Joss. Carlos." Ferg Ferguson was standing up in the farthest booth, waving them over. Primo's was filled with its usual mixture of families, Gallaudet University students using sign language, young adults, and Cap Central students. Joss and Carlos sat down at a table with their friends.

"You want pizza?" Carlos asked.

"Not yet. Maybe just a Diet Coke," Joss answered. She pulled out her cell phone to text Rainie to join them. She held it for a few minutes, waiting to see if Rainie responded. When she didn't, Joss put the phone back in her purse.

Unconsciously, she shook her head in exasperation.

"Trouble?" Durand Butler asked as he sat down at the table.

"I don't know," Joss said. "I hope not. I was texting Rainie to see if she could join us. But she's not answering."

"You know she's at work, right?" Durand said.

"Oh! No, actually, I didn't know that," Joss answered. "Are you sure?"

"Yeah, I just walked her over there," Durand said.

"*Really?*" Joss said slowly with a smile. "Interesting."

"Is it?" Durand asked, looking amused.

"How well do you know her?" Joss asked.

"I've known her since we were kids," Durand said. "We've always been in classes together."

"Does she seem different to you lately?" Joss asked.

"Oh yeah!" Durand grinned. "She sure does!"

"You're hopeless," Joss said, shaking her head. "I actually meant something more serious."

"Like what?" Durand asked, the smile gone.

"Not sure yet. Just keep an eye on her, okay? I've been wondering if there's something wrong."

Durand was quiet for a moment. Then he grinned again. "Oh, I can keep an eye on her."

"I hear that," she said with a laugh. Just then, her cell phone signaled a text message.

"Can't get away—Freezee craze."

"She's not coming," Joss said.

"Honestly, I'm not sure what you're worried about. But I'll pay attention," Durand said more seriously.

"Thanks," Joss said. "She's a good friend. And something's not right."

"I'm gonna get a soda. Anybody need anything?" Durand asked, getting up from the table.

Joss watched him leave. *Hmm, Rainie and Durand. It makes sense in a lot of ways*, she thought. *And it wouldn't hurt to have someone else watching over her.*

"I know that look," Carlos said softly. "You're plotting something!"

"Rainie and Durand. What do you think?"

"Works for me," Carlos said with a laugh.

RAINIE

FreeZees was busy all evening. Durand stuck his head in as he had promised, but Rainie was too busy to do anything more than wave. When the last customers finally left, it was after eleven. Rainie was glad to hang up her apron.

"That was crazy!" Angie Stewart, the manager of FreeZees, said as she wiped up the last table. "I think we went through about a hundred pounds of toppings. I never even took a break. Did you get dinner tonight?"

"Sure, I took a break," Rainie said. She had taken a break but hadn't eaten anything. Instead, she walked up and down H Street a few times, then came back in.

"You want a ride?" Angie asked as she did most every night Rainie worked. Although just a few years out of school herself, she often acted like Rainie's mother.

"You know I'm okay with taking the bus," Rainie said. "It's not far."

"Well, I worry about you," Angie said. "And you know what? Tonight I'm gonna insist on driving you. It's late, girl. You don't want to be out there by yourself."

Rainie was glad for the ride. Truth was, she hated the trip home. The street lights made long, spooky shadows. Sometimes when she was walking home from the bus stop, she saw men hanging around some of the empty storefronts that lined Bladensburg Road. She was always relieved when she reached her house.

As Angie pulled up in front of her house, Rainie's heart fell. Daymon's beat-up old car was parked out front. The car was an ugly shade of green. It had one black fender.

"Is that Daymon Jenkins's car?" Angie asked, leaning forward to look out the front window.

"Know anyone else with an ugly car like that?" Rainie asked angrily. "You know he dates my mother, though they never seem to go on any actual dates."

"He is bad news, sister," Angie said. "I knew a woman he was dating. He borrowed money and stole from her. By the time she finally kicked him out, she was just so glad to be rid of him that she almost didn't care."

"He scares me to death," Rainie said. Something about sitting in the dark car with someone who knew Daymon made the words pour out of her. "My mother dresses really tacky now that he's around. I hate him. He's always looking at me as if he could see through my clothes."

"Is that why you wear long sleeves and stuff?" Angie asked. "I wondered what was going on. I actually wondered if ... well, never mind."

"What?" Rainie asked. "What were you going to say?"

"I wondered if you were maybe hurting yourself. Like cutting."

"He's not worth the scars," Rainie said with a bitter laugh. "I just don't know how to get my mother to see what trash he is. She won't talk about him. It's like as soon as she started dating him, my sister and I quit mattering to her."

"Well, sweetie, if you ever want to talk or need a safe place to hang, you just give me a call, okay?" Angie said kindly. "Seriously. You have my cell phone number."

Rainie felt tears spring to her eyes. "Okay," she said. "Thanks."

She opened the car door, and Angie said suddenly, "Wait! My gosh, what's wrong with me? I can't remember anything these days." She banged her head on the steering wheel. "Corie decided she can work Saturday night after all. So you wanna just work ten to four? I know I told you that you could work that night too, but it being Saturday ..."

"Ten to four is good. Corie can have Saturday night," Rainie said quickly. This way she could sleep over at Eva's. And maybe see Durand Butler if the guys came over.

"Sounds good. See you tomorrow," Angie said.

Rainie opened the door. "You're the best," she said. "Thanks for the ride."

She unlocked the door and walked in as quietly as she could. She put her backpack on the floor, walked upstairs, and went into the bathroom to wash up. When she opened the door to leave, Daymon was standing directly in front of her. She screamed in fear, and he clapped a hand over her mouth.

"Don't make any noise. You don't want to wake up baby sister," he whispered. "Now where were you? It's late."

"I was at FreeZees," Rainie said. "Not that it's any of your business. And where's my mother?"

"I'm making it my business," he said. "Your mama's still at work. I came over here to watch li'l sis until you got home. Thought you'd be home long before this. You think I don't know that place closes at ten? Maybe your mama don't care you be stayin' out late, but I do."

He still had his hand over her mouth, but he moved it down so that he was stroking her chin.

Rainie jerked her head away from him. "Don't you *dare* touch me, you creep," she said.

"Or what?" Daymon asked with a sneer. "Who you gonna tell? Your mama? And what you gonna say? I surprised you. You were about to scream, and I hushed you up so Jesika wouldn't wake up. Why you gonna make it something it ain't?"

"Get out of my way," she said, trying to move around him.

Instead, he blocked the door by leaning

against one side of the jam with his arm on the other side. "Who's stopping you?" he taunted her. "Move me out of the way, if you can."

"Sissy? Is that you?" Jesika called. The little girl came out of her room, squinting her eyes against the light. "I heard something."

Daymon turned at the sound of her voice, and Rainie used the opportunity to step around him.

"I'm just getting home," she said. "C'mon. Back to bed." She led Jesika down the hall to her bedroom. Once inside, she locked the door and lay down beside her in the bed.

"Are you sleeping in here tonight?" Jesika asked sleepily.

"At least for a while," Rainie whispered.

"I hate Daymon," Jesika said softly. "I wish Mom had never met him. I miss Dad, don't you?"

"I do, Jessie. I really do," Rainie said. She put her arms around her sister and snuggled against her. Jesika soon fell asleep. A short time later, the front door closed. Rainie hoped that meant Daymon was gone, but she was too scared to go out and check. She spent the night locked in Jesika's room, still wearing the clothes she'd worn to school.

CHAPTER 10

JOSS

As she got ready for bed that night, Joss thought back over the day. Her thoughts again turned to Rainie. Maybe her friend was just having a bad day. But the more Joss thought about it, the more it seemed like there had been a string of bad days.

Sure, there was the eating thing. Rainie's refusal to eat wasn't normal. When they'd worked together during the summer, they had eaten together lots of times. They often ended their shift at FreeZees with a bowl of frozen yogurt. Rainie used to cover her yogurt with chocolate chips, then ladle hot caramel sauce over the whole thing, making a soupy, sweet mess. She didn't overeat, but she never would have turned down as many meals or snacks as she did today.

But it was more than just the eating. Rainie was withdrawn and very quick to get angry. This was *not* normal for her. She had always been cheerful and easy to get along with. Rainie was a good friend, and Joss was worried. Joss knew she could just leave Rainie alone while she worked out whatever was bothering her. But she cared too much for her friend to give up.

She picked up her phone and called Rainie's cell. It rang and rang. When it finally went to voicemail, Joss hung up without leaving a message.

She wondered where Rainie was. She hoped she hadn't decided to take a run that late at night. Their neighborhood wasn't safe enough for a girl to run by herself after sunset.

Joss tossed and turned. She wanted to help but didn't know how. She needed to talk to someone who knew how to handle this kind of thing. Immediately, one name came to mind.

Mrs. McArdle.

She'd talk to her in the morning. Hopefully, she would know what to do.

RAINIE

The next day, Rainie ran into Durand a few blocks from school.

"Hey, how are you?" he said with a big smile when he saw her. Rainie had never noticed how warm his dark eyes were or how long his lashes were.

"Girl, I get hot just looking at you," he said.

Rainie's eyes widened in surprise.

"Oh my gosh!" Durand looked horrified. "I didn't mean ... I just meant ... you wear such warm clothes, and it's so hot out. I get all sweaty when I look at you! I mean, I just—oh, shoot. I didn't mean any of this the way it sounded."

He looked so embarrassed that Rainie had to laugh. "So you meant hot, but not *hot*? Is that what you're trying to say?" she asked with a smile.

"Yeah, I mean, you look good. Great, actually. But I wouldn't have said—"

"It's okay," Rainie said. "I knew what you meant ... I mean, really ... it's me. We've known each other since we were five." She couldn't read the look that crossed his face.

"Right. I wouldn't have wanted you to think—"

"Oh, I don't. I didn't," Rainie said quickly. She wasn't even sure what she was reassuring him about.

They walked in silence for a few minutes.

"So did you ever Google the name of that guy?" Durand asked.

"We don't have the Internet at home," Rainie said.

"Go to the library at lunch and use the school's computers. Maybe you'll find out that he's an ax murderer or something. Then your mom will quit dating him."

"Gosh, I hope so. That'd be great!" Rainie said enthusiastically. She realized how silly it was to be hoping that her mother's boyfriend was an ax murderer, and she started laughing. Durand laughed too.

They walked into school together. At the door, Rainie stopped suddenly.

"Hey, is wrestling like self-defense?" she asked.

"Kind of, I guess," he answered. "I mean, someone's coming after you, and you try not to let him get you down on the mat. And the whole point is to keep from getting pinned down. If you can pin the other guy, that's even better. Why?"

"What if the guy is bigger than you are?" she asked.

"That's why wrestlers wrestle guys in their weight class," Durand answered. "But there are some tricks that would work even if someone was bigger than you. You thinking of joining the team?" he asked. "I hear Cardozo's got a girl wrestler. Monica something. None of the guys were sure where to grab her at first, but now they just treat her like one of the guys."

"Not on the school team, no," Rainie said.

"I can see you're thinking about something," Durand said. "MMA? They have women's leagues, you know."

"Do you do mixed martial arts too?" Rainie asked.

"Yeah, that's mostly why I wrestle," Durand said. "I do MMA on the weekends. Wrestling keeps me in shape and helps me with some of the MMA moves. You want to practice some moves, you just let me know."

"I will," Rainie said. "Thanks!" She turned and started walking toward her locker.

"I'll just bet he could show you some moves!" Eva joked, walking up beside her.

"Oh, stop!" Rainie said with a chuckle. She went to first period feeling better than she had in a long time.

JOSS

Joss got to school early. She immediately went to Mrs. McArdle's classroom.

"Joss, good morning! What's up?" the English teacher asked as she wrote on the whiteboard.

"Mrs. McArdle, if I ask you something, do you have to pass on the information?" Joss asked.

"Depends on the information," Mrs. McArdle said. "I have to pass on anything that indicates that a student is in danger from themselves or from another person. I'd love to hear what's on your mind, but you need to know what the law requires me to do."

Joss made a face. "I'm not sure what to do here," she said.

"Is this a problem you're having? Or someone else?" Mrs. McArdle asked.

"Someone else," Joss said. "Does that change things?"

"Sort of," Mrs. McArdle said. "Why don't you try telling me what's on your mind but without using a name. I can't report it if I don't know who it is."

"Sounds fair," Joss said. "Okay, what if you had a friend who all of a sudden changed—drastically. Her appearance is lousy, she's not acting like herself, her grades are slipping. Would you think something bad was going on?"

"Yes, actually I would," Mrs. McArdle said. "Have you asked her?"

"Yes, but she has all sorts of excuses for what's happening. I just don't believe them," Joss said. "I think ... I'm not really sure what I think. I just know it's not right."

"You can tell the school counselor, and she can talk to her," Mrs. McArdle offered. "But chances are, if she's not talking to you, she's not going to talk to Mrs. Blackwell either."

"I know," Joss said. "But I'm really worried."

"Can you talk to her parents?"

"Not really," Joss said. "There's just a mom. I

don't know her at all, and of course she'd end up telling Rai—I mean, my friend."

Mrs. McArdle nodded knowingly.

Joss was certain her teacher knew she'd almost said Rainie's name.

"I guess all you can do is let her know you're there for her," Mrs. McArdle said. "I know that's not a great answer. But unless she's willing to tell someone what's going on, it's about all you can do. Just be her friend. Don't judge. And keep the lines of communication open in case she does feel like talking."

Joss nodded. "Thanks," she said.

CHAPTER 13

RAINIE

As soon as it was lunch, Rainie ran to the library. She logged in to one of the computers. She opened Google and typed "Daymon Jenkins" into the search box.

She immediately got a hit. A news article dated two years earlier reported that Daymon Jenkins of Washington, D.C., had been arrested for having a relationship with a student. The article did not identify the victim, except to say that she was a student at Coolidge High School, where Jenkins worked. A follow-up article said that he was cleared of all charges. The girl wasn't underage. She refused to cooperate with the investigation.

Rainie was excited. This was just what she needed to prove to her mother that Daymon was dangerous. She downloaded the articles onto her flash drive. She left the library feeling righteous. As soon as her mom got home from work, she was going to show her what she'd found.

That night, Rainie didn't argue when Angie offered to drive her home.

"Oh, you see what I don't see?" Angie said as she pulled up to the curb.

Rainie looked around for Daymon's car but didn't see it. "Yeah, no Daymon," she said. "Good. 'Cause I need to show my mother what I found out about him."

She told Angie about the news articles she'd found on Google. Angie shook her head in disgust. "Girl, I told you he was bad news," she said. "He's not even good-looking. I don't know why any woman would want to have anything to do with him."

"I think he makes my mom feel pretty," Rainie said. "She took it hard when my dad left. She quit caring about how she looked, and she just lay around the house watching TV. But then she got the job at the bar, and he started hanging around. I think that having a guy like her—even a low-life like Daymon—makes her feel like she's still got it going on."

"Well, looks like you've got the night off from his ugly company," Angie said. "Thanks for working, and I'll see you bright and early tomorrow morning. All right?"

"Yep. Ten o'clock. See ya!"

Rainie unlocked the door to the house and opened it. Her mother was asleep on the couch in front of the television. Rainie tiptoed to her room, put down her backpack, and changed into her pajamas. She came back down and sat on the couch. She knew it would wake her mother up, but she really wanted to have a chance to talk to her.

"Hmm, Rainie, baby, is that you?" her mother asked sleepily.

"Yeah, sorry I woke you," Rainie said. "Did you work tonight?"

"Things were slow at the bar, so DC let me come home early. Do you want something to eat?"

"I ate at work," Rainie lied. "Before I forget, Mom, can I sleep over at Eva Morales's house tomorrow night? She and Joss and I have to finish our science project."

"Will her parents be home?" Mrs. Burkette asked.

"I'm sure they will be, but you can call if you'd feel better about it," Rainie said.

"That's okay, baby. I trust you," her mother said. "I'll see if Daymon can stay with Jessie."

"Oh no—Mom, you can't!" Rainie cried.

"What are you talking about?" her mother asked curiously.

"Mom, I have to tell you something," Rainie said slowly. She knew her mother wouldn't like what she was about to say. "I went to the library today and I ... I looked something up."

"What did you look up? You know you could have asked me about anything. Was it about where babies come from? We've talked about this before, but if you have questions—"

"Mom ... no, just listen," Rainie said. "I looked up Daymon's name on Google."

Mrs. Burkette's mouth opened and closed as if she wanted to say something, but nothing came out. "You did what?" she said finally.

"I looked Daymon up on Google," Rainie repeated. "Mom, he makes me so uncomfortable. What do you know about him? Who *is* he? I just wanted to know if there was anything about him on the Internet. And I found something. He was charged with abusing a kid."

"You're lying!" Mrs. Burkette hissed. "I know all about Daymon. He's told me all his secrets. That's what people do when they care about each other. He would have told me if something like that were true."

"Mom, it is true. I can prove it. I have the articles here," Rainie jumped up and stuck her flash drive into the computer. "Here, I'll show you."

"I don't even want to see," her mother said. "I don't believe you."

Rainie was crushed. Her mother had called her a liar. She'd rather defend Daymon than believe her own daughter. She watched the computer screen, and when the list of files appeared, she opened one of the articles she had downloaded.

"Here," she said. "Read this. He was arrested for messing around with a girl at Coolidge when he worked there."

"Then why isn't he in jail?" her mother asked.

"Because they couldn't prove it," Rainie said.

"She refused to cooperate. But I'll bet that's why he quit working there."

"You know, anyone can make up anything and put it on the Internet," Mrs. Burkette said, not looking at the computer screen. "But that doesn't make it true. Daymon's an attractive man, and I'm sure he was a target for the girls at that school."

"Mom, you've got to listen to me," Rainie said in despair. She took a deep breath. It was so hard to try to convince her mother that her boyfriend might be dangerous. "I don't like being alone with him, Mom," Rainie said softly. "I think he wants to, to—"

"To what? Spit it out, girl. You've gone this far," Mrs. Burkette said coldly.

"He looks at me funny, and sometimes he touches me when he shouldn't," Rainie whispered.

"Touches you? Where?"

"Last night, he touched my chin," Rainie said.

"Your chin?" her mother said with a laugh. "Girl, I think you're safe. I've never heard of chin abuse! Your chin," she repeated bitterly. "I know what's going on here. Daymon's a little younger than me, and it bothers you to have a good-looking young man in the house. You're thinking of him in a way you know you shouldn't, and—"

"Mom!" Rainie yelled, jumping to her feet. "That's a lie. He makes me sick, and you make me sick for letting him come around here. I hate him. Something bad's going to happen, and you won't even listen to me."

"Girl, you watch how you speak to me," her mother said sternly. "Daymon is the best thing that's happened to me since that lousy father of yours took off. And now you want to ruin it. This conversation is over."

Rainie ran upstairs to her room. Without even turning on the light, she threw herself on her bed and started sobbing. She was terrified. She knew Daymon was evil. The one person who could protect her—who *should* protect her— refused to admit there was a problem. Somehow, Rainie had to figure out how to protect herself and her little sister.

CHAPTER 14

JOSS

Joss was glad that she and Rainie were sleeping over at Eva's that night. She hoped she would have a chance to talk to Rainie about her concerns.

Her phone rang in the afternoon. She saw that it was Eva.

"Hey, what snacks do you want tonight?" Eva asked. "My mom's going shopping."

"Oooh! Cheese curls!" Joss said. "And get some candy!"

"What do you think Rainie wants? She's working at FreeZees, so I can't reach her."

"I'll bet she wouldn't tell you even if you could reach her," Joss said. "I don't think she eats anymore."

"I know, right?" Eva said. "She's gotten really,

really skinny. She pulled up the leg of her pants to scratch her leg in class yesterday. I couldn't believe what her leg looked like. What is wrong with her? Do you think she's sick?"

"I don't know," Joss said. "Maybe we can find out tonight."

"Bring your stuff to my house, and let's go to Primo's," Eva said. "Ferg said the guys were eating dinner there."

"Sounds good," Joss said. "Make sure you text Rainie. I don't know how anyone could resist Primo's pizza."

RAINIE

Rainie jumped in the shower and dressed in jeans and a loose-fitting, long-sleeved shirt. She headed downstairs to the kitchen and ate half a banana. She buried the rest in the bottom of the garbage can so her mother wouldn't find it.

"Sissy, come watch 'My Little Pony' with me!" Jesika called from the living room. She was curled up on the couch, watching cartoons. Rainie sat down and pulled her sister close. Jesika meant more to her than anyone in the world. The thought of Daymon alone with her was frightening.

"Jessie, has Mom ever talked to you about what to do if someone tries to, to—" Rainie didn't know what words to say to warn the younger girl about being touched inappropriately.

"Shhh. This is the good part," Jesika said without taking her eyes off the screen.

Rainie waited for a commercial and muted the TV. "Listen, Jessie, this is important," she said. "There are bad people in the world who like to mess with kids. Sometimes, they're people you know. If anyone ever tries to touch you in places that should be private, do whatever you can to keep him from doing it. Kick him, scratch him, scream—whatever, okay?"

Jesika looked horrified. "Mom would kill me if I did that to anyone!" she said. "It's against the law."

"Actually, it's against the law for somebody to touch you like that," Rainie said. "I'm not talking about nice people giving you a hug or somebody kissing you who you like. This is someone besides Mom or a doctor. Someone wanting to touch you where your bathing suit goes. The police have said that you can hurt them bad for doing that," she said.

"Why are you telling me this?" Jesika said with a frightened look. "You're scaring me."

"Rainie, aren't you supposed to be at work?"

Rainie's mother padded downstairs and into the living room, rubbing her eyes.

"I'm about to leave," Rainie said. She was still hurt over her conversation with her mother the night before. She didn't want to talk to her now. "I'll go straight to Eva's after work. So I won't see you till tomorrow."

"Okay. I've decided to ask Mrs. Walker if she can watch Jessie for me tonight."

Rainie turned and looked at her mother. Her mother was looking down at her fingernails. She looked up and gave Rainie a little half smile.

"Thanks, Mom," Rainie said. She hugged her mother. Tears came to her eyes, and she brushed them away. "I love you, you know."

Her mother patted her on the back. "I love you too, baby," she said. She pulled away with a puzzled look. "Hey, have you lost some weight?"

"Oh, maybe a little," Rainie lied. "I've been running a lot."

"Well, don't get too skinny. Guys like us curvy girls."

"Who cares what guys like, Mom?" Rainie

said in exasperation. "I want to look the way I want to look."

"Fine. I don't want to fight with you," Mrs. Burkette said, fixing herself a cup of coffee. "Have a good day at work, and have fun at Eva's. I'll see you tomorrow."

Rainie kissed her mother on the cheek and ruffled Jesika's hair. Grabbing her backpack, she left for work.

JOSS

Here we are!" Joss called out from the back booth at Primo's.

She was sitting in a booth with Carlos, Eva, Ferg, and Durand. She waved Rainie over. "Slide over!" she whispered to Eva. Eva slid toward the wall, leaving space for Rainie beside Durand.

"Dang! I hoped you'd be wearing that cute little apron!" Durand said, moving over to give her more room.

Rainie rolled her eyes. "As if I'd ever wear that thing in public!" She laughed. "How long have you guys been here?"

"Just got here. We waited for you before ordering. What do you like on your pizza?" Joss asked.

"Anything you want is fine with me," Rainie said.

The waitress came to the table and took their order.

"So did you guys work on science today?" Joss asked the guys.

"We meant to," Ferg said.

"Yeah, but it quit raining, and one thing led to another, and before we knew it ..." Durand said.

"They shot hoops all day," Eva said, rolling her eyes. "Blew off the whole day."

"Hey, I told you it wasn't our fault," Carlos said. "We were walking toward the library, and my uncle drove by. He was on his way to the Trinidad Rec Center and told us he needed players. So it's his fault!"

Carlos's uncle was a police officer who coached basketball at the rec center.

"So who played?" Joss asked.

"Some guys were there from Coolidge, and then some others from Cap Cent showed up— JaQuel Rivas, Jair Nobles, Luther Ransome, Chance Ruffin, that freshman Tyrell Wilkins— just a lot of guys," Durand said.

"I can never figure Jair out," Eva said.

"I know, right?" Carlos said. "One day, he'll be trying to prove he's a stud by trying to punch anyone around, and the next day he's okay. Today was one of the good days."

"Good thing too!" Ferg said. "I don't have enough eyes to watch Jair as well as Luther and Chance. They're the ones I don't trust. At least Jair's not sneaky. But Luther and Chance? They're dirty."

"I hear that!" Rainie said. "They came into FreeZees the other day, poured themselves huge cups of yogurt, and never paid. Chance even dumped his on the floor, and I had to clean up after him."

"What a pig," Joss said.

"They cheat, and lie, and do anything they can to get ahead," Carlos said. "Seriously, if one of their grandmothers were in the way of what they wanted, they'd run her right over. There'd be tire marks down her housedress!"

The girls laughed at the image.

"Luther's the smart one, and he gets Chance to do his dirty work," Durand added. "I don't know if it's true, but I've heard that Chance has stolen tests for Luther so he can keep his grades high enough to stay eligible for sports."

"I never understood why they haven't gotten caught," Eva said in disgust. "Everyone knows they're cheaters."

"Wish they'd get caught," Ferg said. "Just not during football or basketball season," he added with a laugh.

"Wait, back to your plans for the day," Rainie said. "I'm a little confused. So you guys were on your way to the library but got waylaid, right? Did you have all your science stuff with you when you played ball?"

No one answered.

"You are such liars!" Joss yelled. "You were never going to the library."

"And here I was so impressed," Rainie said when she quit laughing.

Right then, the waitress showed up and put two large pizzas on the table.

"Saved from any more confessions," Durand said. "Man, I'm starving!"

He helped himself to two pieces. "What kind do you want?" he asked Rainie.

"Just give me one of those," she said, pointing to the pepperoni pizza and sliding her plate over.

Durand put the slice on her plate. Soon it was quiet, as they all tore into their food.

Joss watched Rainie pinch off a piece of cheese. She played with it without eating it.

"Aren't you going to eat that?" Durand asked as he reached for another piece.

"It's still a little hot," Rainie said. She looked as if she took a bite but wiped a napkin across her lips. Joss could swear she spit the pizza into the napkin. Rainie did this with the rest of the slice until only the crust was left.

"Mmm, I'm stuffed," Carlos said when the last piece was gone.

"Me too! I love Primo's pizza," Ferg added.

"How about you?" Joss asked Rainie. "Are you full?"

"Mmm. I'm stuffed. That was great!" Rainie answered.

Joss shook her head at the lie.

"So what'll we do now?" Rainie asked.

"Let's sit on the hill and watch the sun go

down," Eva said. Cap Central sat on a slight hill. Students liked to sit behind the school building and look out over Washington, D.C., as the sun set.

"Shotgun!" Ferg yelled, racing toward Eva's car. He got in the front seat, and Carlos and Joss got in the back.

"Good thing you drove, Butler!" Carlos said to Durand. "There's not enough room for you and Rainie in Eva's piece of junk."

Durand turned to Rainie. "So you want to ride with me?" he asked, pointing to a red coupe parked behind Eva's car.

"Sure."

"Hey, you two," Eva yelled out the window. "Don't get lost!"

Rainie waved, and Eva closed one eye in an exaggerated wink. Rainie rolled her eyes and got in Durand's car.

RAINIE

When did you get this?" Rainie said, looking around the car. In the back were a pair of sneakers, a basketball, and a hooded sweatshirt.

"It's actually my grandfather's," Durand said. "He can't drive anymore, so he lets me drive it. I guess I've sort of taken it over."

"Great for you, I guess," Rainie said. "Not for him so much."

"Yeah, it was sad when he gave me the keys," Durand said. "My mom was glad. She freaked at the thought of him still driving. So now I take him to doctor's appointments and other stuff. I spend time with him whenever I can."

Rainie was touched. "That's really nice," she said, smiling.

"He means a lot to me," Durand said. "I used

to spend almost every weekend at my grandparents' house when I was little. After my grandma died, he was really lonely, so I try to keep him company."

He pulled into the Cap Central parking lot and pulled in next to Eva's car. Ferg was taking a folded quilt out of the trunk.

"We call bench!" Carlos said. There was one bench behind the school. It was usually occupied by a couple. Those not lucky enough to grab the bench usually just sat in the grass. The best spot for enjoying the view was obvious because the grass was trampled down.

Eva and Ferg spread out the quilt. Eva sat down, and Ferg stretched out beside her. Rainie felt awkward. She didn't know if she should sit on the blanket or in the grass.

"You want to learn some moves?" Durand asked her. "It won't hurt if you fall on the grass."

"Sure!" Rainie said. "MMA or self-defense or something. Just how to get away from someone who's grabbing you."

"They're pretty similar," Durand said. "Different legal moves. But basically the same. Okay, so come at me, and I'll show you some tricks."

Rainie pushed at his chest. He didn't budge. "Okay, well, this isn't going to work," she said. "You have to pretend to be me."

Durand put his hand on his hip and the other in his hair. "How's this?" he said in a high voice.

"I never look like that," Rainie said, laughing. "Just quit being so ... so, you know. Unmovable."

"Okay. Just come at me and grab me."

Rainie put her arms around his chest and tugged, trying to make him fall. He still didn't budge.

"See? You can't be a nice person if you're gonna win," Durand said. "Wrestlers start with one kneeling on the mat and the other standing up, but you'll never find yourself in that position. So you need to learn how to disable a guy. Or better still, how to get away. If someone was attacking you, you just want to get away. How about if I take you down, and you try to escape?"

Rainie nodded and braced for his attack. He bent her over his arm, and using his legs, kicked her legs out from under her. She fell back onto the grass. For a moment, her breath was knocked out of her.

"Shoot! Sorry, are you all right?" Durand

asked, falling to his knees beside her. He looked concerned.

"I … I'm fine," Rainie whispered. Durand's face was so close, she could feel his breath. Her eyes seemed to be locked on his, and she couldn't look away.

"Still want to work on escaping?" he asked softly.

No, she thought. *I want to stay here forever.* "I probably should," she said instead.

"Dang!" Durand said with a shaky laugh. "Okay, don't actually do it, but you know you can always knee somebody, right? Like, where it hurts. You can also push against somebody's throat or his eyeballs. Bite, spit, whatever. There are rules in MMA and wrestling, but if you're in trouble, there aren't any rules."

Rainie sat up. Durand stood up and reached his hand down to help her to her feet. They walked over to the blanket. Joss and Carlos had joined Eva and Ferg. The blanket wasn't too big, and there was not much space left to sit.

"Homes, don't even try to sit over here," Carlos said, shoving Durand toward Rainie. "There's no room over on this side."

Durand sat down. He reached up to Rainie and pulled her down so that she was sitting between his outstretched legs, her back against his chest.

"You've got grass in your hair," he said softly, pulling it out gently.

Rainie felt like she couldn't breathe.

"Thanks," she said.

He folded his arms around her and held her close.

"Okay, everybody, get ready!" Eva said excitedly. "The sun's almost down."

In the distance, they could see the busy streets of Washington. The national aspects of the city and its famous people could have been thousands of miles away. To them it was just D.C., their hometown.

As the last of the sun dipped below the horizon, Carlos stood up. "And that's all, folks," he announced, clapping his hands together.

The others stood up. Rainie and Durand shook out the blanket. They folded it, and Rainie handed it to Eva.

"So are we coming over to your place?" Ferg asked Eva.

"Nah, we gotta work on our project," she said. "And so do you guys. You gotta get a good grade on it. It's the only thing that's gonna pull your science grade out of the toilet."

"Yeah, between science and math, I'm in big trouble," Carlos said. "English ain't so good either."

" 'Ain't'?" Joss repeated in disgust. "No wonder you're failing!"

"I'm not failing, I'm just not doing so good this semester," Carlos said.

"It's like everyone needs help this year," Ferg said as they reached the cars.

Rainie kept quiet. She didn't want anyone to know how much trouble she was in with her grades.

"Okay, Butler, I guess we're going with you," Carlos said. He kissed Joss and got in the car.

"See you later," Ferg said. He quickly kissed Eva and gave her a hug. "Study hard, ladies!"

Rainie's eyes met Durand's. He gave her a big goofy grin and blew her a kiss.

JOSS

The girls got into Eva's car. Joss turned around in her seat to face Rainie.

"Still say there's nothing going on with you and Durand?" she asked with a laugh.

"I don't know where that came from," Rainie said, shaking her head. "Must have been the sunset."

"I'll tell you where that came from," Eva said. "Girl, he's in love. You can just tell from looking at him."

"Oh, please," Rainie started. "We've been friends since—"

"Well, you're more than friends now," Joss said, turning back around in her seat. "And I give you my blessing, by the way."

"Me too!" Eva said. "You guys look really cute together."

"We'll see," Rainie said.

Eva pulled into a parking place in front of her house on the corner of Nineteenth Street and Lang Place. The car was crooked and stuck out into the street.

"Nice parking job!" Joss said sarcastically. "Are you going to straighten it out?"

"Nah," Eva said, locking her car. "My dad will be taking it to work soon. It won't be here long."

She opened the front door. A chubby, naked toddler was sitting on the floor of the living room. The little girl grinned when she saw Eva and ran over with her arms outstretched.

"Oooh, how's my baby sister?" Eva said, picking the girl up. "Ma, Carmen is naked again!" she yelled. "She needs a diaper before she has an accident."

A young boy ran into the room, then ran over to give Joss a hug.

"Hey, Diego!" Joss said, kissing the top of his head. "How's my favorite little guy?"

"Big little guy! I'm your favorite big little guy," Diego said.

"You're right," Joss said with a laugh. "You are my favorite big little guy."

"Evie! Evie!" a little girl yelled, throwing herself into Eva's arms. "Can you play Barbies with me?"

"Not now, Tina," Eva said, kissing her. "We have work to do."

"Ma?" Eva yelled. "Ma? We're home!"

Joss had to laugh at the look on Rainie's face. "A little overwhelming, isn't it?" she said.

Rainie nodded, her eyes wide.

Mrs. Morales came out of the kitchen, wiping her hands on a dish towel. "Okay, okay," she shouted. "You don't have to shout at me. Hello, Joss. Nice to see you. And you must be Rainie," she added in a friendly way.

"Sorry," Eva said, untangling the arms of her younger siblings from around her legs. "Ma, this is Rainie. Rainie, Ma."

Right then, a puppy came running into the room and had a little accident on the floor.

"No, no, no!" Mrs. Morales said, picking up the squirming mess. "I told your father if he kept this dog, he'd have to clean up after it. Now where is he? Mario? Mario? The dog peed again."

She started to walk out and turned back to the girls. "Sorry," she said. "We must look like crazy people."

"That's because we *are* crazy people," a deep voice said. A big man with huge forearms walked in the room and took the puppy from his wife. "Hello, girls. Joss, how are you, *chica*? Rainie, glad to meet you. I'm Evie's dad. Sorry about the mess," he said with a laugh. "We've got two here who aren't housebroken. I suspect the dog will learn his manners before the baby."

As if she knew she was being talked about, Carmen gave a big smile.

"Come on, let's go to the basement and get out of the chaos," Eva said. She led the way through the kitchen and down the basement stairs.

The basement was filled with a washer and dryer, old toys and furniture, an ancient television, and two worn couches. Eva switched on the TV and flopped down on one of the couches.

"Make yourselves at home," she said. "I share a room with Tina, so we'll stay down here tonight."

"Your family seems nice," Rainie said.

"They're okay. They make me crazy, though," Eva said. "And I worry about my naked baby sister. She won't wear clothes. Everything we put on her she takes right back off."

"She'll grow out of it," Joss said with a wink.

"Hey, wanna see our scum?" Eva said, jumping up off the couch. "It's over here." She walked to a dark corner of the basement. On a shelf were four bowls covered with mold.

"So none of the antibacterial soaps kept mold from growing," Joss said. "What do we do about that?"

"It's still okay," Rainie said. "It's still a conclusion, even if it's not what we expected. Want me to start taking notes?"

"I want to get in my pj's first," Eva said. "It's really hot down here. Plus, I want a snack." She started for the stairs. "I'll be right back. You guys can get changed in the bathroom down here if you want." She ran up the wooden basement stairs. Her heavy footsteps echoed.

Joss wondered whether Rainie would change out of her jeans. "Do you want to get changed first?" she asked. She thought she knew what the answer would be.

"No thanks, I'm good," Rainie said, as expected. "You go ahead."

Joss didn't want to let it drop. "You are going to change, though, right?" she asked. "I mean, it is awfully hot down here."

"Whatever," Rainie said.

Joss narrowed her eyes. She looked at Rainie for a long moment without saying anything. "Suit yourself," she said finally as she turned to go into the bathroom. "I'll be right back."

Soon Eva came thumping down the stairs carrying bags of potato chips, tortilla chips, and cheese curls. "I didn't know what you liked, so I made my mother buy it all," she said, ripping open each bag.

Joss came out of the bathroom wearing shorts and a T-shirt.

"Mmm, looks good," Joss said, eyeing all the food. "What looks good to you, Rainie?"

"Oh, all of it," Rainie said.

"Um-hm," Joss said skeptically.

"Well, I'm starting with the cheese curls," Eva said. "Here, want some?" she offered, handing the bag to Joss.

"Sure," Joss said, taking a handful. "How about you?" She handed the bag to Rainie.

"Great, thanks!" Rainie said. Joss watched her closely. Although it sounded like she was grabbing a large handful, when she pulled out her hand, she actually only had a few cheese curls in it. She started to munch on one, taking little bites with her front teeth.

"Anybody want a Diet Coke?" Eva said, walking over to the beat-up refrigerator humming in the corner.

"Sure!" Rainie said.

"I'll take one too," Joss said. "Unless you've got something else in there."

Joss walked over to the refrigerator. As she turned back around, she saw Rainie put something under the couch. When Rainie saw that Joss had seen her, she looked guilty. She reached for the bag of cheese curls and pulled out another handful. Again she made a big show of munching the snacks while actually only taking little bites.

"I'm going to wash my hands," Rainie said, heading toward the bathroom.

As soon as the door shut, Joss turned to Eva. "We have to say something," she said. "She's only pretending to eat. We've got to help her, or tell her to get help or something."

"Go for it," Eva said. "I'm with you on this one."

When Rainie came back, she looked from one girl to the other.

"Okay, what's up?" she asked. "I can tell you were talking about me."

Joss took a deep breath. "We're worried about you," she said. "We think you might be anorexic."

Rainie's jaw dropped. "*What?*" she asked.

"We think you have anorexia," Eva said. "You never eat, you run all the time, and you've lost a ton of weight. It's not normal."

"Look, I just don't eat snacks and pizza like everyone else. But that doesn't mean I have a problem," Rainie said. "I'm just not hungry. I eat so much at FreeZees, and I—"

"Stop," Joss said. "Quit lying. Something's up with you, and we want to know what it is. You've changed, and we're worried."

"Well, thanks. But you can quit worrying.

I'm not anorexic. I just don't live for food like the rest of you do."

Eva looked hurt. "Was that about me? Because I'm fat?"

"I didn't say you were fat," Rainie said. "Food's just not important to me, that's all."

Joss wasn't willing to let it go. "I don't believe you," she said. "How much do you weigh?"

"I have no idea. We don't own a scale," Rainie lied. "Anyway, how much do *you* weigh?"

"One hundred twenty-five pounds," Joss said. "There, I've told you, so you tell me."

"Like I said, I don't even know," Rainie said.

"My mom has a scale upstairs," Eva said. "You can weigh yourself on it."

"Seriously?" Rainie said. "I'm not playing this game. I don't have a problem, okay? Now just drop it!"

Joss took a deep breath. "No," she said. "I'm not going to drop it. I care about you, and I'm telling you the truth. You look bad, and I think you have an eating disorder. Prove me wrong. Get on the scale so you can prove that you weigh a normal amount."

Rainie was quiet for a moment. "Okay, but I

don't want anyone to look," she said. "I'll weigh myself and tell you what it says, okay?"

"Let's go!" Eva said. They all climbed the basement stairs and went up to the bathroom on the second floor. A pink scale sat on the floor. Rainie walked into the bathroom and shooed the others out.

Joss and Eva heard the scale scrape along the bathroom floor as if someone stepped on it.

"You know she's going to lie, right?" Joss whispered.

Eva nodded. "Guess we didn't handle this too well, did we?" she said.

The door opened. "One hundred twenty-seven," Rainie announced.

"I don't believe you," Joss said.

"Whatever," Rainie said coldly. "I did what you asked me to do. Now let it go."

They went back downstairs to the basement. In their absence, Eva's little brother and sister had come down and were munching on cheese curls.

"Oh, great!" Eva said. "Now everybody's down here." The puppy emerged from under the couch, licking cheese curl dust off his face.

"Hmm. Looks like he discovered some cheese curls under the couch. I wonder how they got there," Joss asked, looking at Rainie.

"Maybe I dropped one," Rainie said lamely.

"Maybe you did," Joss repeated.

Eva shooed out her two siblings and the puppy, then latched the basement door securely.

She turned on a movie on the TV and shut off the lights. Soon she was asleep. Joss got up and turned off the TV.

"Are you sleeping in your clothes?" she whispered.

"Yes," Rainie whispered back.

"I won't be able to see you if you want to get changed to sleep in pj's," Joss said.

"I actually didn't bring any. I always sleep in my clothes," Rainie said.

"So no one sees how skinny you are?" Joss asked.

Rainie didn't answer.

"Look, I'm your friend. And I'm really, really worried about you," Joss said. "People have died from anorexia. They can have heart attacks. I don't know why you're starving yourself, but something is clearly wrong. If you can't talk to me about it, talk to someone. What about your mom?"

Rainie's laugh was bitter. "She's the last person I can talk to," she said.

"What about Mrs. Blackwell?" Joss asked. "Or Mrs. McArdle? Someone. This isn't healthy."

"Look, I appreciate that you are worried about me," Rainie said. "I just wanted to lose a little weight, that's all. I've got it under control," she added.

"Fine," Joss said. She rolled over so her back was to Rainie. "But you're going to need to talk to someone sooner or later. So you should start thinking about who that's going to be."

Rainie didn't answer.

In a few minutes, Joss thought she heard Rainie crying softly. She felt frustrated and sad. She didn't know how to help her friend.

CHAPTER 19

RAINIE

It wasn't possible to sleep late at Eva's house. From the basement, the thumps and squeals were proof that the three younger kids were up and active.

"Just once, I'd like to be able to sleep all morning," Eva said with a groan. "This must be what it's like to live in a zoo."

Rainie didn't mind the chaos. It sounded like fun compared to the tension in her home. She missed being a family, with a dad like Mr. Morales, who she knew would kick the butt of any guy who tried to pull the stuff Daymon was pulling.

"Girls, I made homemade donuts," Mrs. Morales called down. "Come on up now; they taste best when they're hot."

"Let's go!" Eva said, throwing off her quilt and standing up. "My mom's donuts are the best."

"They smell great!" Joss said, following Eva up the stairs. She stopped and looked at Rainie. "Are you coming?" she asked.

"Of course," Rainie said. In the confusion that was the Morales's breakfast table, no one noticed that she ate little of her donut.

When breakfast was over, she put on her backpack and thanked Eva.

"You're walking home?" Joss asked.

"It's not far," Rainie said. "I don't mind."

"Whatever," Joss said coldly.

Rainie knew Joss was still angry. But there was nothing she could do.

When Rainie got home, she went straight up to the bathroom to take a shower. After getting dressed, she opened her agenda book to see what homework she had to work on. She had just settled onto her bed when there was a knock at the door. She opened it to find Daymon leaning against the frame, wearing only underwear.

"Seriously?" she said, not even trying to hide her hatred.

"Where were you all night?" he said with a leer. He stuck his foot inside the door so she wouldn't be able to close it.

"Not that it's your business, but I was at a friend's house," Rainie said.

"I'll bet you were! What's his name?" Daymon asked.

Rainie didn't even bother to answer. She tried to close the door, but Daymon's foot held it open.

"What do you want?" Rainie said. "I need to get some schoolwork done."

"Thought you might need some help in here," Daymon said. "I'm pretty good in math."

"Thanks. I'm good," Rainie said. She kicked his foot and shoved the door closed with a slam. "And put some clothes on before Jesika wakes up!" she yelled through the door.

She shivered in disgust. She wished she had somewhere else to live. But even if she did, she would never leave Jesika with this creep. If their mother couldn't—or wouldn't—protect her daughters, at least Rainie could protect her little sister.

She felt too distracted to concentrate on

homework. She knew she had lots to make up, though, so she looked over her agenda book to see what was due and what she'd missed.

- Math: five missed assignments
- English: Shakespeare project due Tuesday
- US History: test Monday, causes of the War of 1812
- Science: Display boards for science projects due Friday

Plus the poms meeting Monday night and working ... How would she ever get it all done?

She settled down to get to work. Before she could get started, loud music started playing downstairs. She opened her bedroom door and went down to the kitchen. Daymon had hooked up some speakers and was dancing to the music.

"Like it?" he asked. "Got 'em for next to nothing."

"Stole them, in other words," Rainie said, shouting to be heard above the music.

"Got them from a friend of mine down in Prince George's County," he said. "I didn't ask where they came from."

Jesika came into the room, rubbing her eyes. "Sissy, why are you playing music?" she asked sleepily.

"What are you doing?" Mrs. Burkette asked, bursting into the kitchen. She looked accusingly at Rainie. "Are you out of your mind? Do you know what time I get home from work? I'd like to get some sleep."

"It's not me!" Rainie yelled. "It's Daymon! Why do you always take his side against me?"

She turned and ran upstairs to her bedroom, slamming the door. Through the door, she could hear the music, a little softer but still throbbing.

She gathered her homework up and shoved it into her backpack. She'd never be able to work with the noise. Fortunately, the public library was open on Sundays.

She caught a bus near her house. In the quiet of the library, she made some progress. She turned off her phone so she wouldn't lose focus. She finished all her math assignments and put them in her "turn in" folder. She'd been using this system since elementary school and it had always worked—when she actually did the assignments.

The Shakespeare project was too open-ended. "Research a topic relating to life in Shakespeare's day. Then find evidence of that topic in his plays and discuss."

Rainie thought of several topics but discarded them all. None seemed interesting enough or easy enough to get done in the amount of time she had available.

She sat at one of the library's computers and typed various search terms into Google and Wikipedia. Her stomach felt empty—a feeling she had come to enjoy. It meant she was resisting the temptation to eat.

That gave her an idea. She wondered what people in Shakespeare's day ate. She entered "Elizabethan food" into Google and got several hits. Scrolling through the websites, she saw that she'd be able to find lots of information. She entered "Shakespeare food" into the search box and got even more hits.

She knew she had found her topic. She began doing the research.

By the time the library closed at five, Rainie had made progress on most of her schoolwork. She even had a basic understanding of the causes of the War of 1812. As she waited for the bus, she turned her phone back on. It rang immediately. She didn't recognize the number.

"Hello?" she said.

"Hey, it's Durand," a familiar voice said. "I was about to go for a run, and I wondered if you wanted to go too."

"Sure," she said. "I'm not home right now. Give me forty-five minutes." She could see the bus approaching.

"Sounds good. Meet me at the school bike rack?"

"I'll be there," Rainie said.

As she walked up the front steps to her house, she could smell barbeque sauce. Her mouth began to water. Opening the door, she saw Daymon in front of the TV. She heard her mother banging around in the kitchen.

"What's going on?" she asked as she walked into the kitchen.

"Daymon asked some friends over for dinner. I'm broiling some ribs," her mother said, wiping sweat off her forehead.

"Daymon asked *his* friends over, but *you're* cooking?" Rainie asked. "What's Daymon doing?"

"Drinking a beer," Daymon yelled. "And you'd better watch your mouth, girl. Don't you be taking an attitude with me!"

"Mom, why do you let him talk to me that way?" Rainie asked softly. "He's not my father!"

"Oh, Rainie, can't you just grow up?" Mrs. Burkette said with a sigh. "Honestly, he's trying—it's you who's the problem."

"Seriously, Mom?" Rainie said, tears springing to her eyes. "Seriously? I guess you've made your choice."

She ran up to her room and cried hard for a few minutes. Then she blew her nose, changed into her running clothes, tip-toed downstairs— Daymon and his friends were laughing it up in the kitchen—and slipped out the front door.

Durand was waiting when she arrived at the school.

"Hey, you okay?" he asked, looking at her with concern.

"Yeah, why?" she asked.

"Your eyes look funny," he said. "Like you've been—never mind."

"I'm fine," she lied. "I was just up late last night at Eva's."

"Sure," he said, sounding unconvinced. "Anyway, what route do you take?"

"Follow me," Rainie said as she started running up Maryland Avenue.

They soon found a pace that was comfortable for both of them, allowing them to talk while they ran. It was a comfortable conversation about school, homework, their friends. Whenever the topic of family came up, though, Rainie changed the subject.

After about a mile, she started to feel more tired than usual. She slowed down, and Durand slowed with her. As they neared the National Arboretum, Rainie felt things start to spin.

"Whoa!" she gasped, nearly going down. She stopped and put her arms out to try and steady herself. "Everything's spinning!"

"Here, hold on to me," Durand said, putting his arm around her. "Let's sit in the grass where it's cool."

He led her over to a grassy hillside. It was almost dark. Most of the tourists had gone, so they had the place to themselves.

"I love this place," Rainie said. "It's like a little piece of heaven in D.C."

"I know," Durand said. "I run here as often as I can. It's so much better than running on the main roads."

Rainie lay in the grass and shut her eyes.

"You okay?" Durand asked after a while.

"Yeah, I don't know what happened," Rainie said. "I felt like I was about to faint."

"Maybe you're not eating enough," Durand said. "I get like that during wrestling when I'm trying to make weight."

"Maybe," Rainie said noncommittally. "Do you ever feel like giving up?" Rainie asked.

"You mean, like kill yourself?" Durand asked with concern.

"No, not like that. Just give up. Just say, 'I give up. I'm not going to care anymore.'"

"Do you feel like that now?" Durand asked.

"I feel ... I feel ..." Rainie couldn't go on.

"How?" Durand asked gently.

"Like there's this huge, horrible thing ... this force pulling on me so hard that I can barely stand up to it. Like it's going to pull me in, and something terrible is about to happen."

"School? Family? Life in general?"

"Daymon Jenkins," Rainie said, tears again coming to her eyes.

"So he's still hanging around?" Durand asked.

Rainie nodded miserably.

"Sorry," he said. "I guess your Google research didn't turn up anything you could use to make your mom dump his sorry ass."

"It did, actually, but she didn't believe it. She didn't believe me," she whispered.

"I'm sorry," Durand said again gently. "That must have hurt. But the longer she's with him, the better the chances that she'll see him for the loser he is."

"I can only hope," Rainie said, sitting up. "But meanwhile, it's getting so that I can't stand being home when he's there."

"No wonder you run so much," Durand said, moving a stray hair from her face. "If there's anything I can do ..." his voice trailed off.

"Thanks," Rainie said. She stood up and brushed the grass off her pants. They slowly started walking back toward their neighborhood.

After a quiet few minutes, they stopped in

front of Rainie's house on Seventeenth Street. Durand put his hand on her arm. "You know, there are a lot of people who care about you. Who would do anything to help you," he said gently.

"Thanks," Rainie said distractedly, looking around for Daymon's car.

"Like me, for instance," he continued.

Rainie heard something in his voice and looked at him. His eyes were kind, but there was something else there, something she hadn't seen before.

"See ya," he said. He bent down and kissed her on the lips.

His kiss left Rainie speechless. It felt so good—soft and hard at the same time.

"You're lots more fun to run with than the wrestling team," he added with a grin. Then he waved and walked on down the street.

Rainie turned and went into the house. For the first time in a long time, she felt happy.

JOSS

Joss woke up early, filled with excitement. The first poms practice was after school.

After the last bell, she headed for the girls' locker room to change. Everyone changed into T-shirts and shorts except for Rainie. She kept on her long pants and sweatshirt.

Mrs. McArdle came in and looked them over. "Rainie, you're going to die of the heat," she said. "Did you forget to bring practice clothes?"

"Yeah," Rainie said with a laugh. "What an idiot, right? I'm okay, though. I'll bring them next time."

"Anyone have any clothes they can lend Rainie?" Mrs. McArdle asked. Several girls put up their hands.

"I'll be fine," Rainie said firmly. "Really."

"All right, let's get started," Mrs. McArdle said. "Want to practice some moves first or go over business?"

"Moves!" the girls shouted.

"Okay, but first you have to stretch and warm up," Mrs. McArdle said. She led them in some stretching exercises. She made them run four laps around the perimeter of the gym. She then showed them some basic steps. She turned on the music, and they tried doing them in unison. They were terrible—not in sync, turning in opposite directions.

After practicing for a while, Mrs. McArdle said, "Okay, that's enough for one day. Do one lap around the gym, and then let's talk."

The girls all started running around the gym. Joss looked back and saw that Rainie was at the rear of the group. Joss got out of line and circled back to run beside her friend. She didn't like how Rainie looked. She was sweating and seemed to have difficulty running in a straight line.

"Rainie? You okay?" Joss asked.

"I'm … I'm …" Rainie started to say. She stumbled a few steps, then stopped. Her eyes closed, and she sank to the floor.

"Rainie!" Joss yelled. She squatted down beside her.

"Mrs. McArdle, come quick! Rainie fainted!"

Mrs. McArdle ran over to Rainie, who was now surrounded by all the girls.

"Stand back, girls. It's probably the heat. Someone get some cold water."

Two girls ran to the drinking fountain and took turns filling their water bottles. Joss pulled up Rainie's sweatshirt.

"Oh my gosh! She was wearing another shirt," she said. "Why didn't she take off the top layer?" She pulled up both to try to cool Rainie down.

What she saw made her gasp. All of Rainie's ribs stuck out, along with her hip bones. She wasn't just thin, she was emaciated.

Joss and Mrs. McArdle exchanged a look.

"Where is that water?" the teacher said finally.

One girl handed her a water bottle. She poured some on her hand, and then rubbed Rainie's forehead and neck. She also poured a little on Rainie's stomach. Soon Rainie's eyes began to flutter.

"What happened?" she asked, trying to sit up.

"You fainted," Mrs. McArdle said. "Probably the heat. Let's take off your sweatshirt."

She bent down to help pull the sweatshirt over Rainie's head.

"No!" Rainie cried, trying to hold onto the sweatshirt.

"Yes," Mrs. McArdle said sternly. "The rest of you, go get changed. Practice is over for the day."

The other girls started to leave. Joss could hear them all talking excitedly about what had happened.

"You too, Joss," Mrs. McArdle said kindly. "I'll take it from here."

Joss didn't want to leave, but she knew she had to. She left the gym and grabbed Eva.

"We need to find Durand," she said.

RAINIE

Whc gym got quiet as the poms team left. Rainie continued lying on the cool gym floor. As soon as the sweatshirt was off, Rainie felt better. The air hit her skin and cooled her down. She knew her secret was out.

"Rainie, I'm going to have to tell Mrs. Hess about this," Mrs. McArdle said gently. "You're in trouble, and you need to get help."

"Because I fainted from the heat? I should have taken off my sweatshirt, I realize, but—"

"Don't lie," Mrs. McArdle said. "Something is very wrong. I suspect you have an eating disorder. You've been trying to hide it, but you can't any longer. You need to see a doctor, Rainie."

"Please, Mrs. McArdle," Rainie said. "Don't do this to me." She angrily wiped away some tears.

"Honey, I'm trying to help you," Mrs. McArdle said. "You're killing yourself."

She pulled out a cell phone. "I'll call your mother to come pick you up," she said.

"You won't be able to reach her," Rainie said miserably. "She's at work."

"I can't hold you here," Mrs. McArdle said. "But I'm sure the school will be in touch with her. Rainie? You must get some help. Understand?"

Rainie nodded and stood up. She was still a little unsteady on her feet.

"How are you getting home?" Mrs. McArdle asked. "You can't walk in this condition."

"I can take her," Durand Butler said from the door of the gym. Rainie could see Joss and Eva behind him. "Joss told me what happened," he said to Rainie. "I'll drive you home."

"Thanks, Durand," Mrs. McArdle said. "And, Rainie, remember, I'm not the enemy here."

Rainie nodded, too miserable to speak. She and Durand walked out of the gym toward the parking lot.

"So I guess everyone knows my secret, right?" Rainie said bitterly. "Like it was anyone else's business."

"If it makes you feel any better," Durand said. "We'd all pretty much figured it out before you passed out. Joss and Eva have been very worried about you."

"They should mind their own business," Rainie said, opening the door of Durand's car.

"Well, they didn't do anything to get you in trouble," he said, turning the key. "They were just keeping an eye on you. But when you faint at school, that's pretty much a red flag."

"My mother's going to kill me," Rainie said. "She's going to think I'm just trying to get attention."

"I doubt that," Durand said. "Mrs. McArdle will make her take it seriously."

They pulled up in front of the house. "You want me to come up?" he said.

"Nah, probably best if you don't," Rainie said. "I've got to face her myself at some point."

She was relieved to see that Daymon's car wasn't outside. Her mother wasn't home either.

Mrs. Walker was watching Jesika. Rainie thanked Mrs. Walker and locked the door behind her. Then she went straight up to her room. She knew the school did not have the phone number for DC's bar, so she had some time before Mrs. McArdle reached Mrs. Burkette.

In the morning, Rainie quickly got dressed and went to school. She went straight to first period without talking to anyone. About twenty minutes after the class started, Mrs. Dominguez, the principal's secretary, called on the class phone. She asked Rainie to come to the office. Rainie gathered up her books and put them into her backpack. Her heart felt heavy.

As she walked toward the door, Durand got out of his seat and joined her at the door.

"Whatever happens, I'm here for you," he said quietly. "You know that, right?"

Rainie couldn't even bring herself to speak. She nodded and gave him a half smile.

The walk down the hall to the main office seemed to take forever. Rainie didn't know what the school would do to her. She opened the door to the office, and immediately Mrs. Dominguez picked up the phone.

"Rainie Burkette is here," she said into the phone.

"Rainie, how nice to see you," said Principal

Hess as she walked out to the waiting room. "Why don't you join us in my office?"

Us? Ugh! Like I have a choice, Rainie thought to herself. She reluctantly got up and followed Mrs. Hess into her office. She stopped abruptly at the door. Sitting around the principal's desk were Mrs. McArdle; Mrs. Blackwell, the guidance counselor; and her mother.

"Rainie, you're not in any trouble," Mrs. Hess started. "But we need to talk to you about something serious. Do you know why you're here?"

"Yeah. I passed out yesterday at poms practice because it was so hot in the gym, and Mrs. McArdle decided it meant I had an eating disorder."

"Don't get smart!" Rainie's mother snapped.

"Mrs. Burkette, please," Mrs. Hess said kindly. "Why don't you let us handle this? When we're done talking, you can say whatever you feel needs to be said."

Mrs. Burkette settled back into her chair. Her body language showed how angry she was.

"Rainie, do *you* think you have an eating disorder?" Mrs. Hess continued.

"No!" Rainie said sharply. "I've lost a little

weight, but I'm totally in control. Every girl at this school wants to lose weight. Why am I in trouble? Just because I'm the only one who was actually successful?"

"Rainie, I know a bit about eating disorders. I had one myself when I was in high school," Mrs. Blackwell said. "I know the signs. What did you have for dinner last night?"

Rainie was caught off guard by the question. "Um ... leftover ribs," she lied.

"She's lying," Mrs. Burkette said softly. "There weren't any leftovers. I left her some spaghetti, but I don't think she ate any."

"How many nights a week do you run?" Mrs. Blackwell asked.

"Just a couple," Rainie said.

"She runs every night she's not working at FreeZees and for long times on the weekends," Mrs. Burkette said sadly. "Oh, I'm so stupid. How could I not have known?"

"Don't blame yourself, Mrs. Burkette," Mrs. Blackwell said. "Kids with eating disorders become very adept at hiding them. Rainie's a smart girl. She knew how to hide it from you. But that brings up another issue: how are things at home? Any stress there that could be contributing to this situation?"

"Well, her father took off a year ago," Mrs. Burkette said. "And—" she turned and looked at Rainie. In that look, Rainie could see that her mother understood the role that Daymon Jenkins was playing in Rainie's life. "And there are other stresses as well," her mother said. "I guess I didn't realize how much it was affecting her."

Rainie appreciated how hard it must have been for her mother to admit this. Everyone was quiet for a moment.

"Unfortunately, we can't allow Rainie back in school until we get a note from her pediatrician," Mrs. Hess said. "She is physically unstable. She fainted yesterday. I'm sure you understand why she should not be in school until your family doctor says it's okay."

"What?" Rainie gasped. "No way. I don't need to go to the doctor. I keep telling you I'm okay."

"Rainie, I've heard enough. I'm taking you to the doctor," her mother said as Rainie glared at the group.

"There are many free counseling services I can refer you to, Mrs. Burkette," Mrs. Blackwell said. "Your family doctor can help determine what—if any—further treatment is necessary. And, Rainie, you can return just as soon as your doctor pronounces you fit to attend school."

"Fit to attend school?" Rainie asked incredulously. "Where else would I go? None of this has anything to do with school!"

"And you need to discuss that with your doctor," Mrs. Hess said firmly. "I've let all your teachers know that you may be out of school for a few days. Here are all of your assignments. Do you have all your books?"

"Yeah, I've got everything I need," Rainie said, standing up. "And good luck with the poms team," she said to Mrs. McArdle. "I sure would have liked to have been a part of it."

"And I'm hoping you still can," Mrs. McArdle said gently. "But you need to get healthy first."

"Thank you for looking out for my girl," Mrs. Burkette said, standing up. "I'll make the appointment today so Rainie doesn't miss too many days of school."

Mrs. Hess guided mother and daughter out of her office. Mrs. McArdle accompanied them through the school hallway. As soon as they got to the entrance, Mrs. McArdle gave Rainie a hug.

"You're going to be okay, Rainie," she asserted. Then she shook Mrs. Burkette's hand and walked away, leaving mother and daughter alone.

Rainie and her mother walked to the parking lot. "What are we going to do?" Rainie asked bleakly.

"We'll figure something out," her mother said. "But those ladies were right. We need to get you healthy. With everything else going on, I guess I lost track of what you were eating and how much you were running. I feel like such a failure as a mother."

"It's not about you," Rainie said. "You've got your own stuff to deal with. And anyway, I still don't think I have—"

"Stop, Rainie," her mother said. "Let's quit the lying right now. Let me see your arm."

"No," Rainie said.

"Do it. Now," her mother said in a voice that didn't allow for any disobedience.

Rainie slowly pushed her sleeve up. Her

wrist bones stuck out, and her forearm was the size of a stick.

"Oh my gosh," her mother said, her voice catching. She opened her car door and waited for Rainie to get in the other side.

Rainie's mom whipped out her cell phone. In minutes, she was explaining her daughter's situation to someone at the doctor's office. An appointment was secured for that afternoon. Mrs. Burkette glanced at her daughter and patted her on the knee.

They didn't talk as they drove home. When they pulled up, Rainie saw Daymon's car.

"Oh, great," Rainie said. "Mom, I just don't know if I can face him this morning. Any way you could get rid of him for a while?"

"I don't actually know why he's here," her mother said curiously. "He had asked if I would be around, and when I said I wouldn't be, he made it sound like he had something he needed to do."

They got out of the car and walked up the steps to the front door. Rainie's mom put the key in the lock and turned it, opening the door.

"Daymon?" she called. "Honey, are you here?" She walked upstairs with Rainie following closely behind her.

The door to her bedroom opened just a crack. "What are you doing home?" Daymon asked, only his face showing. "You said you weren't going to be here!"

"Well, I had to—"

"Daymon, baby, who *is* that?" a woman's voice called out from inside Mrs. Burkette's bedroom.

No one said anything for a long, painful moment.

"Seriously? *Seriously?*" Mrs. Burkette said, her voice rising. "You brought your little tramp to my home?"

She pushed past Daymon and opened the bedroom door. "Get out, you skank!" she yelled. "And you!" she said to Daymon. "Don't you *ever* show your ugly, perverted face around here again! Touching my daughter, pawing me in front of my kids—I should have booted your ugly butt weeks ago!"

"Is that what she told you? She's lying!"

Daymon said, backing further into the bedroom. "I can't believe you'd take that skinny brat's word over mine. And after all I've done for you all."

"I am *so* done with you," Mrs. Burkette said tiredly. "Get your clothes on and get out. I should have listened to my kid."

Rainie and her mom headed downstairs as Daymon closed the bedroom door.

In a minute, he reappeared at the bottom of the stairs, buttoning up his shirt and hopping from one foot to the other as he tried to get his shoes on.

"You really think I cared about you?" he said nastily. "You're about twenty years too old for me, lady. You were just free drinks at DC's and a warm place to stay."

The young woman walked down the stairs. She was tugging a tight knit dress down over her hips. It was so short that it barely covered her underwear.

"But I thought you said this was *your* house," she said, sounding confused.

"Get out. I'll explain it outside," Daymon said. "As for you?" he said to Rainie. "You're about the last piece I would have ever jumped. The right age, but too skinny."

"If you're not out of this house in the next five seconds, I'm calling the cops," Mrs. Burkette said, holding the front door wide open. "One ..."

"Just remember, I—" Daymon started.

"Two ..."

"I need to get my stuff," Daymon whined.

"Three! Rainie, hand me that phone."

"I'm gone," Daymon said, shoving the young woman out the door and slamming it behind them both.

For a long moment, no one spoke. Then Rainie said, "Oh, Mom, I'm so sorry—"

"Stop!" Mrs. Burkette said, holding up her hand. "There is *nothing* to say. He was trash. I was starting to see it before this, and today just convinced me. I am so embarrassed at what a fool I've been."

"You just got a little lost, that's all," Rainie said. "It was hard enough on Jesika and me when Dad left, but you were married to him. I'm sure it made you feel pretty bad."

"I felt like a total failure as a woman," her

mother said. "So when Daymon started acting like I was the greatest thing since sliced bread, I guess I wanted to believe it was true."

"But you *are* the greatest thing since sliced bread," Rainie said, her voice catching. "You're beautiful. Smart. Classy. Unlike that piece of trash that blew in here with Daymon!"

"She was something, wasn't she?" Mrs. Burkette said. "How old do you think she was?"

"No idea," Rainie said. "But that dress was so tight, it's a wonder it didn't cut off her circulation!"

"Was that a dress? I thought it was a shirt, and she forgot to put on her pants!"

"Maybe it was an Ace bandage!" Rainie laughed.

Mrs. Burkette laughed too. "I hope she sprains an ankle falling off those platform shoes," she said.

"He'll dump her when she hits puberty," Rainie said, laughing harder.

"I wonder if he's dating her or adopting her?" her mother said, trying to catch her breath.

"Maybe he's babysitting her," Rainie added.

Mrs. Burkette walked into the kitchen and opened the freezer door. Rainie followed.

"I wonder if he used my microwave to heat her baby bottle?" she said, pulling out a carton of ice cream.

"Maybe he's going to her parent-teacher conference," Rainie said, opening the silverware drawer and pulling out two spoons. She pulled out a chair and sat at the kitchen table.

"Maybe he's arranging play dates for her to meet some little friends," Mrs. Burkette said, sitting in another chair. She put the ice cream container in the center of the table.

"I'm sorry about all this, Mom," Rainie said, suddenly serious. "I didn't mean to worry you."

"Honey ..." her mother started and then stopped. "We're going to be okay," she said. "Both of us."

Mrs. Burkette dug her spoon into the ice cream and pulled out a giant bite. She put the whole thing in her mouth. Then she made a face at how cold it was.

Rainie watched her for a minute, then pulled the carton toward her. "Hey, give me some!" she said as she pulled out a huge spoonful. She started licking the ice cream off the spoon. "Yeah, we'll be okay," Rainie agreed.

ABOUT THE AUTHOR

Leslie McGill was raised in Pittsburgh. She attended Westminster College in New Wilmington, Pennsylvania, and American University in Washington, D.C. She lives in Silver Spring, Maryland, a suburb of Washington, D.C., where she works in a middle school library. She lives with her husband, a newspaper editor, and has two adult children, both of whom have chosen to live as far from home as possible.